THE DELCO YEARS

A car battery is good for five years

THE DELCO YEARS

An interactive graphic novel by Ned Buntline
as CHANNELED through Bill Owens

Illustrations by Francesca Cosanti

4

Contents

The Delco Years

The Delco Years was written in 1999 and put away for 21 years. Then in the Fall of 2020, for some unknown reason (COVID-19), I started re-writing and added illustrations.

Research for *The Delco Years* was done using *Wikipedia*, *Google*, *The New York Times* and the Trinity Foundation. As you read this book, I have provided phone numbers, website links and e-mail addresses for you to verify that the facts as written are indeed true. Do your own searches for the truth.

trinityfoundation.org

I apologize to the hundreds of individuals, companies, and janitorial services that I libeled. I especially apologize if I misspelled your name. I'm ADD-HD and pay AT&T an extra ten dollars a month for "HD."

Any connection to people living or dead is probably intended, but most likely purely by happenstance. This story is true except for the parts I made up.

An interactive novel by Ned Buntline as CHANNELED through Bill Owens

Introduction

We knew as long as we had cars, guns, and cell phones, we could create a new society. We wouldn't slip back to medieval times when men on horseback fought over land, gold, and women. We were not going to "live off the grid," build log cabins or make soap as shown in the *Whole Earth Catalog*. Our coffee was the house blend from Starbucks. When McDonald's quit serving burgers, civilization was over.

The mall now stood empty. I would miss buying Dockers at Macy's. Amazon had disappeared and I could no longer google "looking for love."

Match.com

The short-term plan was simple. With the resources from Costco, Home Depot, and Target, we had at least five years, the life span of a car battery, to rebuild society. No one in our group knew how to kill a chicken or saddle a horse. The reality of one day becoming farmers, herding cattle, and planting crops by the cycles of the moon was real.

A Delco car battery will last five years. We called these the DELCO YEARS.

Chapter 1
King Kong Pizza

On April 15, 2002, an accident occurred at the Boston Logan Airport. A customer, Bobbie Jones, who was at Starbucks, dropped a bottle and accidentally released Anthrax-836. Within 72 hours, the virus circled the globe, and a billion people were infected.

I was drinking an IPA at Buffalo Bill's Brewery in Hayward, California,. I looked out the front window of the pub. Across the street was the Lucky's Supermarket parking lot. I could see numerous shopping carts, and next to them, on the ground, what looked like a pile of clothes.

On ABC News, Peter Jennings was already calling the deadly virus anthrax. In just 24 hours, it had killed more than 200 million people in the USA.

Next to me sat Mitch, Buffalo Bill's chef. He weighed in at 280-pounds and was called "Mr. P." for his personality.

I asked Mitch, "What do you think we should do?"

He responded, "I say let's make a King Kong Pizza."

At 12 pounds, the King Kong was a monster and barely fit into the 40-inch pizza oven. It could feed everyone at the brewery and the nearby Hempery. The Hempery was what some called a "health clinic." Their marijuana must have been good because the employees always ordered the King Kong.

I told Mitch I'd give him a hand and headed to the kitchen. I grabbed five one-pound dough balls and rolled them into a giant pizza ball. Five minutes later, I rolled out the dough.

Mitch applied the toppings: a house-made Italian red sauce, shredded mozzarella, sausage pieces, anchovies, artichoke hearts, Canadian bacon, green peppers, mushrooms, linguica, jalapeño peppers, two cans of Italian sliced tomatoes, extra cheese and topped it off with 96 Hormel pepperoni slices.

Mitch slid the pizza into the 650-degree oven. Ten minutes later, it was ready. With a large pizza cutter, Mitch cut it into 48 pieces. I grabbed the first slice and headed out to the patio.

We watched as looters stripped Lucky's Supermarket and Rite Aid Drug stores. They came in waves of pick-up trucks and SUVs. First, they took the perishable items: Foster Farms chickens, hamburger meat, sausages, pork chops, and T-bone steaks. Next to go were the coffee, tea, olive oil, and Pellegrino Water. Then people made a run on vegetables, bread, bananas, Fritos corn chips, and frozen items like DiGiorno pizza and Eggo Waffles soon disappeared, along with Stouffer's Mac & Cheese, Pepsi, Coke, Arizona Green Monster Energy drinks, canned goods, breakfast cereals, dried nuts, and fig bars.

Finally, one guy showed up in a Ford F-100 pick-up truck. He filled it with toilet paper, bathroom toiletries, mouthwash, hair spray, shampoo, razor blades, dental floss, toothpaste, and household disinfectant products.

The Korean market on Foothill Boulevard was looted. People carried away 100-pound bags of rice, salt fish, tofu, and dried seaweed. Soon everything was gone, including the wooden storage bins. I guess everything in the store became a take-out item.

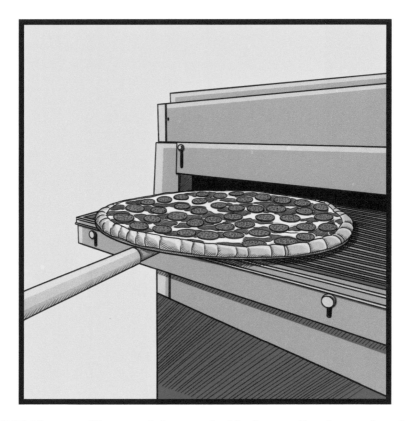

The GNC Nutrition Shop was left untouched by looters. People somehow knew that Krill Oil, Vitamin C, and Herbalife were not part of our future. Looters went into Ace True Value Hardware on B Street and took paint and hand tools.

Across town on Hesperian Boulevard, Home Depot was having a fire sale. Looters arrived in trucks and took everything: lumber, cement, light bulbs, and the kitchen sinks. When the looting was finished, someone set fire to Home Depot and Petco. We didn't need pet food or any GNC products. On the lower end of B Street, Eden Liquors was cleaned out by 9 a.m. People needed alcohol and porn magazines to keep them going. Lotto tickets, *Vogue*, *Rolling Stone*, and *National Geographic* magazines were not essential items.

At Buffalo Bill's Brewery, we drank the last of the wheat beer. The talk turned to how looters had taken large cardboard boxes full of drugs from Longs Drugs and CVS. Then they had used Presto logs and set fire to the store. Over on Grove Street, a few people ransacked the CVS and Rite Aid drugstores. The first item to be looted was Jack Daniel's Tennessee Fire Cinnamon-flavored whiskey. Then bottles of wine and cases of beer were thrown into cars. On the A-list were aspirin, Kaopectate, condoms, and birth control pills.

The blow-up dolls at the 24-hour adult store, L'Amour Shoppe on Main Street, had all disappeared.

The fire spread quickly from Longs Drugs down the block to Washington Savings, People's Legal Aid Service, and Copy Pacific. People ran into the Bank of the West looking for money, only to find the building stripped.

Twenty minutes later, a fire truck came with only two firemen. They rushed into Buffalo Bill's and asked for help. A couple of guys quickly volunteered. I was sure they did it for bragging rights. I knew for sure it wasn't the first time that drunk firemen had saved a city.

The smoke from the numerous fires drifted east, over the hills, towards the Livermore Valley. In just a few days, we would follow the path of the smoke to the Livermore Valley and Wente Winery. I sat at the bar and made a to-do list.

1. Create a mission statement explaining the Viking Rules of Government called the *Althing*. (A Parliament to make laws and rule on matters of justice.)
2. Write a loyalty pledge that each member of the Village will be required to sign to become a citizen of the *Althing* community.
3. Interview individuals who want to join the Village.
4. Get guns from the police department.
5. Clear out any people remaining in shopping malls, city offices, and industrial parks in the Livermore Valley. We will protect the cities from looters.
6. In the control tower at the Livermore Airport, set up a 580 Highway traffic control center. This will serve to keep unwanted settlers, campers, and looters out of the valley.
7. Check out Camp Parks for military weapons and vehicles.
8. Drive out to the Wente Winery to make sure our group could occupy all their buildings.

I asked Tony, Buffalo Bill's bartender, to raid the Hayward Police Department's gun arsenal. He was back in less than an hour with boxes of Glocks, Smith & Wesson, and Bushmasters. Tony let me know he had also cleaned out the evidence room, taking marijuana, drugs, and money boxes.

I looked the other way and muttered under my breath, "Good job, Tony, just what we needed…drugs and dirty money!" I then asked Tony to make one final drive around the Livermore Valley looking for uninvited visitors. I said, "Check for people camping out at City and County Parks, the fairgrounds, and the big box store (Walmart) parking lots. If you find anyone, let them know that the Livermore Valley is now private property. They should either come by Buffalo Bill's in Hayward and apply for citizenship or move along.

And for God's sake, don't shoot at any trespassers! They may have guns and shoot back!"

Around noon, Rod, a Deadhead and the owner of the Avon jewelry store came by the brewery. He'd heard a rumor I was forming a kibbutz of virus survivors. He wanted to check out what I was doing.

I told him that I was going to create a community based on the 12th century Parliament Viking system called *Althing*. The economy of the Village would be centered on bartering wine for goods and services.

Rod wasn't interested in being part of any community, government, or Kibbutz. He didn't get it and suggested he should liberate the San Francisco Diamond Center. Rob then said, "You could trade diamonds for goods and services." I responded, "Just how many diamond rings would you give for a bottle of wine?" Rod walked away. I could tell he just wanted diamonds.

I looked up at the TV and could see somewhere in America a city was burning. It was not my concern. I had to organize a village.

I wanted to check out Camp Parks Army Base for military weapons and vehicles. So I asked Rod to come along. He was an ex-marine, so I assumed he knew something about weapons. When we arrived, the gates to the base were open. We drove around and found most of the buildings were completely empty. In a field nearby, there were rows of High Mobility Wheeled Vehicles (HMWV). I could see a significant problem with using military weapons to defend the Livermore Valley. Rod was the only person who could drive a HMWV and knew how to shoot a stinger missile.

www.military.com/equipment/high-mobility-multipurpose-wheeled-vehicle-hmmwv

Chapter 2

The Fountain of Youth

Larry Bell, the founder of Bell's Brewing in Kalamazoo, Michigan, was sitting at the bar and watching CBS news. The news wasn't good. In one day, a virus had killed 150 million people.

He turned to John Mahler, his master-brewer, and asked, "Why hasn't the virus killed everyone at our brewery?"

John's answer was, "I don't know. Do you want me to phone Final Gravity Brewing and see if their workers are alive?" Larry made the call, and Kevin, a brewmaster at Final Gravity, picked up the phone and said. "Everyone's alive. We're watching the hockey game. Bulldogs up by two!"

Larry had a degree in Biochemistry and had spent a couple of semesters studying the beer yeast, saccharomyces cerevisiae.

He now speculated that maybe there's something in the beer. That somehow, beer drinkers were immune to the virus. Then a brilliant marketing idea crossed Larry's mind. He would trademark the slogan "Drink Beer and Live!" He could make a fortune selling T-shirts.

He opened his laptop, went to *Wikipedia*, and searched the phrase "beer yeast." He quickly found an article published by *American Brewer Magazine* titled "Craft Brewer's Yeast" by Dr. Michael Lewis, UC Davis.

Dr. Lewis' article stated that craft brewers were re-pitching their yeast, batch to batch, and creating super-sized 10-15 micron yeast cells. The yeast cells had developed internal G-proteins pathways, allowing them to join together. They looked like bowling pins. Dr. Lewis' students noted that the supercells looked like Shamoo in Li'l Abner comics.

The Shamoo cells were sending and receiving pheromone (sexual) signals to and from the virus. Then for some undiscovered reason, the Shamoo developed an appetite for the 0.5-micron virus which passed into the stomach and was digested by the e. coli bacteria in the large intestine. Then after a good bowel movement, the craving for beer and pizza returned.

www.cdc.gov/ecoli/index.html

Larry phoned National Public Radio in Boston and asked to speak to known beer drinker Nina Totenberg. On the call, Larry told Nina that all employees and customers at his brewery and the other breweries in Michigan were alive. It was his educated guess that the antidote to the virus was beer, unpasteurized beer!

bellsbeer.com

He told Totenberg there were 2,410 microbreweries in America. He then gave her the phone number (617-456-2322) to the Harpoon Brewery in Boston. Larry suggested she call Harpoon Brewery and see if anyone was alive.

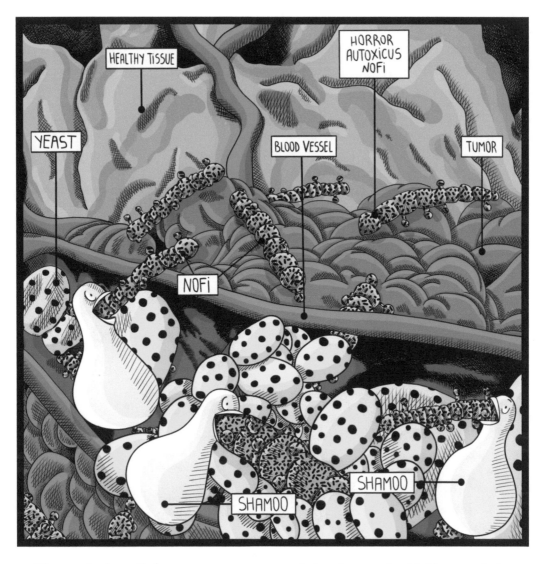

Nina made the call. A young woman answered the phone and said, "Sorry, we're bottling today. No one's free to talk. Call back at 4 pm. I'll find someone to answer your questions."

www.harpoonbrewery.com

Soon public radio stations across the nation were telling listeners to drink craft beer. This information came too late for the majority of NPR listeners, as most were Chardonnay drinkers. I decided to phone all the breweries in Northern California and let them know that I was closing Buffalo Bill's Brewery and, with other virus survivors, forming a new society based on the Viking *Althing*. Our temporary headquarters was at the patio of the Wente Winery restaurant in Livermore. There were 1,000 survivors who were hanging out at craft breweries in Northern California.

There were 180,000 Pandemic survivors at 15 Brewpubs in Northern California. Each brewery would develop its own system of government, including democracy, monarchy, communism, socialism, and oligarchic systems. Only Buffalo Bills would use the Viking Althing form of government.

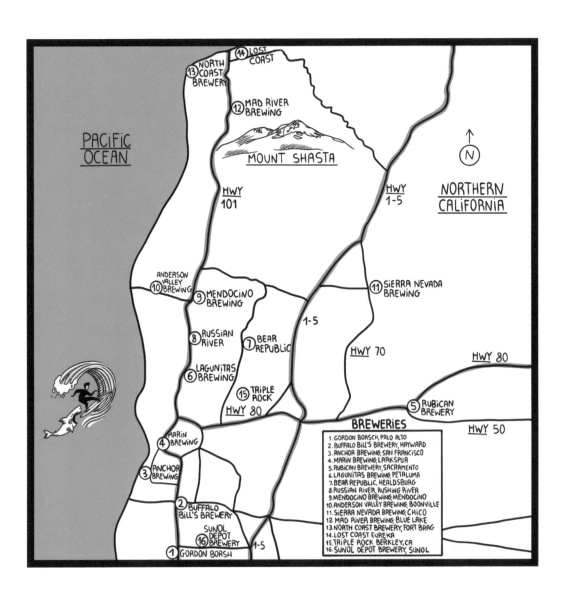

Breweries in Northern California c. 1980

1. Gordon Biersch Brewing	Palo Alto - Dan Gordon, 408-278-1008 *Marzen, Blond Bock & Golden Ale.* Dan said, "I like your idea of building community, good luck."
2. Buffalo Bills	Hayward - Bill Owens, Brewmaster. *Known for Pumpkin Ale and Alimony Ale.*
3. Anchor Brewing	San Francisco - Fritz Maytag, 415-863-8350. *Lager, Pale Ale, Porter and Anchor Steam.* Phone calls went unanswered. Anchor beer was pasteurized.
4. Marin Brewing	Larkspur - Brendan Moland, 415-461-4677 *Ales, Lagers and Stouts.*
5. Rubicon Brewery	Sacramento - Ed Brown, 916-448-4715 *Indian Pale Ale.*
6. Lagunitas Brewing	Petaluma - Tony McGee, FAX 707-763-5252 *Dog Town Pale Ale, IPA, Tocaloma & Bugtown Stout.*
7. Bear Republic Brewing	Healdsburg - Sandy Norgrove, 707-431-7258 *Racer 5, Red Rocket Ale.*
8. Russian River	Santa Rosa - Vinnie Cilurzo. *Piny the Younger considered the best beer in America.*
9. Mendocino Brewing	Mendocino - Don Barkley, Fax 707-477-1015. *Peregrine Pale Ale & Red Tail Ale.*
10. Anderson Valley Brewing	Anderson Valley - Ken Allen,707-895-2337 *Boonville Beers, Boont Amber Ale, Barney Flats Oatmeal Stout.*
11. Sierra Nevada	Chico - Ken Grossman, a pioneer in craft distilling. *The Pale Ale is world famous.*
12. Mad River Brewing	Blue Lake - Robert Smith, 707-668-4151 *Steelhead Extra Pale Ale & Extra Stout.*
13. North Coast Brewing	Fort Brag - Mark Ruedrich, 707-964-3400 *Old Rasputin, Red Seal Ale and Scrimshaw Pilsner.*
14. Lost Coast	Founded by Mark Ruddick. *Brewery Cafe, Beers, Great White and Red Seal.*
15. Triple Rock	Berkeley - (510) 843-2739. *Known for its Lager.*
16. Lyons Brewery Depot	Sunol - Judy Ashworth. "The Beer Missionary" *In 1985 she opened the first multi-tap room in California offering craft beer.*

Chapter 3

Artificial DNA

In 1991 the United States signed the Non-Proliferation Disarmament Treaty with Russia. The Cold War was over, and Russia began to dismantle its stockpile of highly enriched uranium (HEU) and 156 tons of military-grade plutonium.

Very little was known about Biopreparat Research Laboratories, as the labs employed over 55,000 and were scattered all over Russia. Most people had worked on large assembly lines producing tons of deadly pathogens, anthrax, smallpox, and plague. In ten years, Russia had produced enough pathogens to kill the entire world population 100 times over.

In 1972 Russian scientist Dr. Ken Alibek was the Director of the Biopreparat Research Laboratory in Moscow. He made a breakthrough using artificial DNA. He combined the viruses Anthrax and Novskvich using Hemolysin gluing and attached the virus to the flesh-eating Buurli. Alibek had created a new Zoonotic virus, Anthrax-836. It had no known cure. The virus was considered a CHIMERA and was code-named NOFI after his wife's Russian toy dog.

Chimera Pronunciation: /kI' mir-ə Function: noun

Etymology: Latin chimaera, from Greek chimaira she-goat, chimera; akin to Old Norse gymbr yearling ewe, Greek *cheim*.

1 a: capitalized: a fire-breathing she-monster in Greek mythology having a lion's head, a goat's body, and a serpent's tail

b: an imaginary monster compound congruous parts

2: an illusion or fabrication of the mind; especially: an unrealizable dream

3: an individual, organ, or part consisting of tissues of diverse genetic constitution

4: a mixture of the two viruses Anthrax and Novskvich creating a new multi-antibiotic resistant virus Anthrax-836 (or) NOFI. It was deadly and easily transmitted (like smallpox) by coughing.

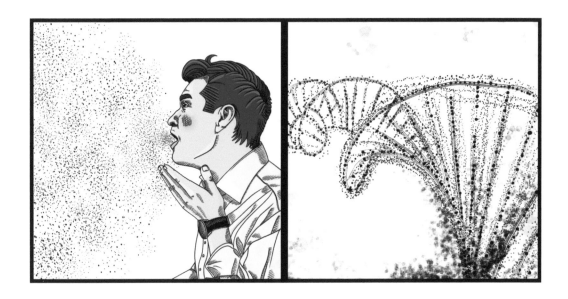

Definitions

Project Bonfire: A Soviet Union development of antibiotic-resistant virus.

Ebola: Flesh eating virus

Horror-autoxicus: Immune system destroying itself

Factor: A virus that copies itself creating a Bonfire

Pathogens: Small Pox, Plague, AIDS, Anthrax and Ebola.

Nerve Agents: Sarin, Agent 33 and VX:

Novichok: Nerve Gas. Anti-crop, Livestock and humans

Phosgene: Choking agent.

Armageddon: "War of the Worlds."

Chimera: A new biohazard weapon combining chemical and biological materials

New Zoonotic Disease: A common mycobacterial infection (Anthrax) transmitted by coughing. Ofter transmitted with ownership of pets.

Ciprofloxacin: Used to treat serious infections. Often used when other antibiotics have not worked Used to treat chest and skin infections.

Military Anthrax: Dried and ground into a 1-5 micron powder that suspends in the air and is easily inhaled. Anthrax is a serious infectious disease caused by gram-positive, rod-shaped bacteria known as Bacillus anthracis.

Eclipse: Treating an Anthrax infection with aspirin making the patient feel better for a few hours.

Pheromones: Proteins that transmit sexual signals joining cells together.

Shamoo Yeast Cells: Super Cells that eat the NOFI virus.

NOFI: A deadly substance, "super sized" virus that kills humans and animals. It is, like smallpox, easily transmitted by humans.

Chapter 4

Sverdlovsk Institute

Anthrax-836 was milled into micro fioli-droplets for testing on the volunteers. Each person was paid $250 to inhale 150 to 12,000 spores per hour, for one to six days. This gave scientists time to study volunteers' immune systems as they fought off the virus and died. Some volunteers were dead within an hour, and others with a strong immune system lived for a week.

Several volunteers inhaled 12,000 spores. They quickly lost control of their central and peripheral nervous systems, experiencing eye and chest pains, difficulty in breathing, and blueish hands. Then pink blisters or vesicles formed on their arms and turned into a black base called an usher. Some volunteers were given aspirin which created what was called an eclipse.

The patient would feel better for a few hours and then die. The sickest volunteers were injected with the antibiotic tetracycline. This created another problem because the tetracycline created peptides allowing the NOFI virus to copy itself speeding up the whole auto-toxic process.

Simply put, the body begins to eat itself. Many people die in minutes; others within a week.

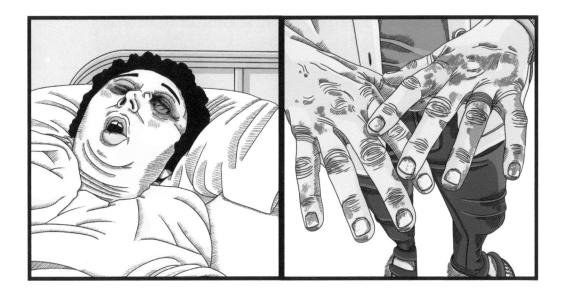

The scene at the Institute was soon horrific, and nothing worked to save the sickest volunteers. After several days of testing, the scientists and support staff were afraid to enter the building.

To make matters worse, the Institute's maintenance crew accidentally opened an exhaust vent on the autoclave. This allowed a large plume of NOFI spores to escape. They drifted to the nearby town of Sverdlovsk and killed 156 people.

en.wikipedia.org/wiki/Sverdlovsk_anthrax_leak

Dr. Alibek ordered 7,000 yards of concrete and had it mixed with calcium hydrochloride, a bleach mixture, to seal off the buildings. At the same time, he demanded that the citizens of Sverdlovsk abandon their city. Six months later, the area looked like a miniature Chernobyl.

Dr. Alibeck created a cover story, saying the NOFI tests were successful, but sadly all the volunteers were killed in a plane crash. The husbands, wives, and relatives of the volunteers received a death certificate, a photograph of the plane crash, and a check for $620.

There was no explanation of what happened to the people living in the city of Sverdlovsk. In Russia, all information about citizens is controlled by the government.

There was one survivor, Herman, a man with German ancestry. He was an alcoholic who drank four to five liters a day of Bitburger, an unfiltered German wheat beer.

On the first day of testing Anthrax-836 (NOFI), Herman suffered from Shigella Dysenteria (diarrhea) so severe that he was removed from the test site and taken to a hospital in Moscow.

ckbo.ru

At the hospital, his daily beer consumption was reduced to two liters. The death of the other volunteers was hidden from him, and a week later, he was given $620 and sent home.

Two weeks later, while visiting the Budvar brewery in the Czech Republic, Herman accidentally drove his car off the road into a river by the brewery and died. This was a major loss for Dr. Alibek's research team because Herman had been scheduled for tests on his immune nervous system.

The development of the NOFI virus and the deaths of the volunteers were hidden from senior military officers and President Gorbachev. Alibek was especially concerned about the Russian military learning about NOFI. He worried they would use bomblets and test the virus on the Ukrainian civilian population.

Alibek's biggest fear was that a single person infected with the NOFI virus would become a vector and create a viral "bonfire." *A bonfire is the result of the multi-antibiotic resistant Anthrax strain made of two different diseases going viral and being unstoppable.*

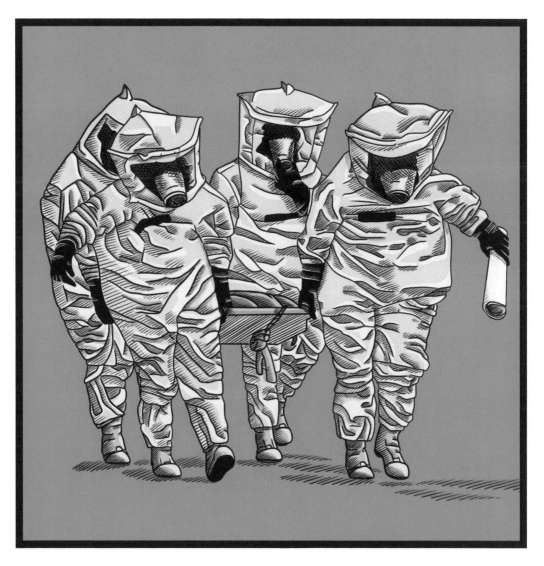

A vector could board an airplane and infect 160 passengers. The 160 passengers would in turn transfer to other airlines and infect 9,100 individuals, who would in turn transfer to 19,000 connecting flights infecting 1,999,900,000 people.

(1 person x160 infections x9100 infections x19,000 flights =1,999,900,000(dead people)

At this point, NOFI would encircle the earth and, in three weeks, kill three billion people. *The only survivors would be people who drank unpasteurized beer.*

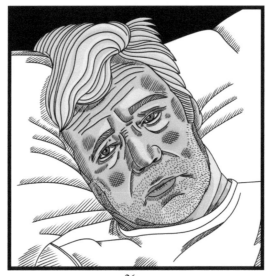

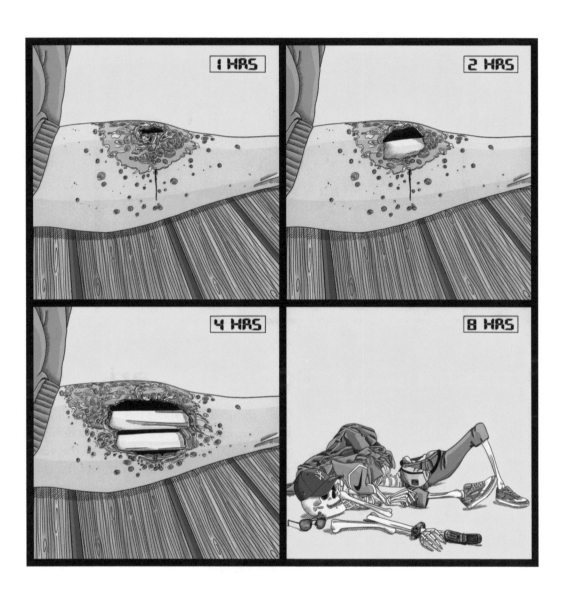

27

Chapter 5
Russian Typhoon Submarines

In the 1970s, American government officials didn't worry about the Russian chemical and biohazard programs. Under President Reagan, the U.S. military installed 3,284 ICBM sites in the states of Michigan, North Dakota, Montana, and Alaska. The government spent additional billions developing the Star Wars program to protect the U.S. from Russian ICBMs.

ips-dc.org/star_wars_revisited_still_dangerous_costly

American spies were not concerned about the Russian biological weapons. The U.S. military calculated that a Soviet missile, launched from Siberia and moving at twice the speed of a bullet, could reach Washington D.C. in sixteen minutes.

ICBMs were, at this point, were worthless. President Reagan pushed to end the Cold War and dismantle the expensive defense programs. In reality, the Cold War had bankrupted the USSR.

During the Cold War, the U.S. Navy had spent more than $400 billion building 80 ICBM-equipped Trident nuclear submarines.

The warheads were aimed at predetermined targets in the USSR. If given the go-ahead by the President, the U.S. military would launch 3,500 land and sea-based warhead missiles in less than eighteen minutes, destroying Russian military bases and flattening all their major seaports and cities. Potential loss of life in less than an hour was estimated at 900 million people.

The main focus of the US Department of Defense was the Russian submarines lying beneath the oceans. These submarines could deliver nuclear bombs to any American city. The US submarines and the Russian fleet had spent years playing blind man's bluff. The Russians were working on drones that could end civilization.

The US scientific community warned the Pentagon that a nuclear attack on Russia would damage the earth's atmosphere and create a nuclear winter. The best-case scenario was that some humans might survive, but the top predators on the earth would be polar bears and alligators. The scientific community wasn't concerned about biological warfare.

In 1972 the opportunity came for Dr. Alibek and his wife to defect to the West. He ordered the destruction of Anthrax-836 (NOFI) and left no notes on its development.

Chapter 6

The Yugo

During the daytime, the only sounds on the Institute's grounds were crows fighting. The security guard had just one set of keys and was paid $300 per month to watch the building. In reality, he performed a once-a-week "inspection" of the building and grounds.

Most of his time was spent sitting in the front office smoking cheap Eastern-European cigarettes. On holidays he smoked Marlboros and drank vodka. On very special occasions, he used the Institute's cafeteria and cooked dinner for his friends and family.

On weekends the guard locked the front gate of the Institute's grounds and went home. The nearby residents were told to keep an eye out for any suspicious activities.

Five years after Boris Yeltsin became president of Russia, the basement of a nondescript office building in the suburbs of Moscow was flooded by the Moskva River. The water destroyed the scientific research papers and the list of scientists who had worked at Biopreparet Institute.

The people who knew about Dr. Alibek's DNA recombinant work on anthrax were now dead or living in the USA.

On February 22, 2002, two bottles of NOFI virus were stolen from the Biopreparet warehouse. The security guard was paid $450 to leave the gates unlocked and look the other way.

With the money, he bought a YUGO and a bicycle for his son.

www.caranddriver.com/features/a21082360/a-quick-history-of-the-yugo-the-worst-car-in-history

He told everyone he had received money from the Russian Army as a settlement for his brother, who was killed fighting in Afghanistan. To celebrate the newly found money, he used the Institute's kitchen and made a large pot of borscht for his friends.

Everyone he knew came to eat, drink and talk about the good old days under Nikita Khrushchev when socialism worked, and people didn't have to work so hard! They longed for the time when vodka was cheap, and you could afford a vacation at the Black Sea.

Borscht Recipe

The Borscht Recipe was handwritten in a small black notebook:

7 gallons of water
8 pounds bone-in beef shank
30 carrots sliced
25 beets, shredded
15 onions sliced
5 heads of sliced cabbage
5 stalks of celery, sliced
10 tomatoes, chunked
10 bay leaves
1 cup salt
1 cup sugar
1/2 cup of vinegar
1 quart of yogurt

Heat 7 gallons of water. Add beef, carrots, onion, bay leaves, celery, and salt. Cover and simmer on low heat for two hours. Let cool, then remove the fat. Add bay leaves, chopped cabbage, chunks of tomatoes, and 1/2 cup of vinegar. Stir in a handful of sugar. Cover and simmer for 30 minutes. When ready to serve, top with yogurt and serve with heavy rye bread.

While the party was going on, the plan to steal anthrax was carried out. Around 8:00 p.m. that evening, a black Mercedes pulled into the Institute parking lot. In the back seat was a Russian Security Officer armed with a Saiga shotgun to provide cover.

en.wikipedia.org/wiki/Saiga-12

The two men sitting in the front of the Mercedes wore gray overcoats, fedoras made in China, and knock-off Italian sunglasses. They looked like characters from a Godfather movie. They smoked cheap cigarettes and talked about World Cup football. They were upset that the Russian football team had become second-rate.

The men studied a map of the building for a few minutes. They got out of the car, opened the trunk, and retrieved a small cardboard box. There were two flashlights in the box, one with dead batteries. They entered the building, soon returned, popped the trunk, and placed two bottles of anthrax inside. The whole operation took less than 20 minutes.

They thought the bottles from the warehouse contained Anthrax coded 22-2022. It was Anthrax, but a different strain. In the semi-darkness of the warehouse, they had taken bottles containing the new Zoonotic disease called Anthrax-836. (NOFI).

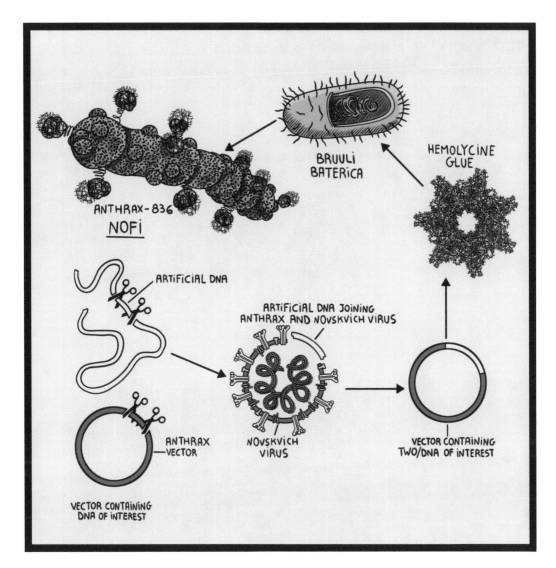

Chapter 7
A New Zoonotic Disease

Dr. Ken Alibek drove a Buick and lived with his wife of 38 years in Alexandria, Virginia. He was a senior fellow at the National Defense University and worked for the Potomac Institute for Policy Studies.

potomacinstitute.org

His PowerPoint lecture on viruses and germs was in high demand at numerous universities and government agencies. He was often a speaker at conferences for Hardin Advanced Biosystems.

www.genomeweb.com

In an interview with The New York Times, Alibek revealed that Russia had developed a low-flying cruise drone equipped with high-pressure nozzles. These drones, if released by

Russia, could spray deadly clouds of aerosolized pathogens over Boston, New York City, Philadelphia, and Washington, D.C.

Dr. Alibek's book, *An Arsenal of Germs*, put the fear of God in the CDC. He claimed that representatives of Osama Bin Laden wanted to buy one thousand military-grade anthrax bomblets.

www.nytimes.com/1999/06/20/books/an-arsenal-of-germs.html

Dr. Alibek lectured at the International Symposium on Protection Against Chemical and Biological Warfare Agents. In one lecture, he revealed that artificial DNA was used to link the viruses Anthrax and Novskvich to the bacteria Bruuli and that his Russian team had created a new Zoonotic virus called Anthrax-836 that had no known cure. He went on to say the Zoonotic Anthrax-836 had the potential to create a viral bonfire, killing most of modern civilization. There was a real chance that civilization would just become hunters and gatherers.

Two months after the 911 terrorist attack on the Twin Towers, Dr. Alibek learned that Anthrax laced letters had been mailed to US Senator Tom Daschle and several media organizations.

en.wikipedia.org/wiki/2001_anthrax_attacks

Alibek knew it wasn't Anthrax-836 (NOFI) because once released, it would copy itself and spread globally.

health.ny.gov/diseases/communicable/anthrax/fact_sheet.htm

He assumed it was a low-grade Anthrax, most likely stolen from Emergent Biodefense Operations in Lansing, Michigan.

www.cdc.gov/anthrax/basics/types/index.html

After living in Virginia for ten years, Alibek and his wife wanted to retire. They wanted to return home to Ukraine. They dreamed of buying a peach farm and keeping bees. His wife missed the hot Ukrainian summer nights and the little yellow watermelons she used to buy at the local open-air market.

At night they drank Grey Goose, a French vodka, and talked about the old days. She ordered garden tools from the Martha Stewart catalog and vegetable seeds from the Burpee catalog. She grew beets, cabbage, and flowers in the backyard. She was ready to return home.

www.burpee.com

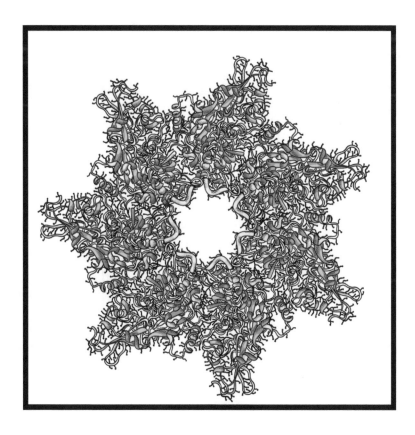

JONES

1911 - 2010

ROBERTO & MARIE JONES

ROBERT

PEARL

TIM

CHARLES

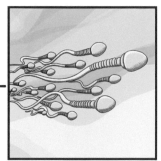

SPERM

BOBBIE

Chapter 8

The Genius Sperm Bank

Robert Graham Jones was born 2/22/73 in San Jose, California. He was raised by Pearl, a single mom. Pearl had been left widowed when her husband, Ralph Elmo Jones, was cleaning the gutters on their house and fell off the ladder. He hit the ground and bounced through the basement window. His body came to a stop with his head resting on a foot pedal of a cast-iron Singer Sewing Machine.

Pearl nicknamed her son Bobbie to avoid people confusing him with her older, well-known second cousin, Dr. Robert Graham. Graham had made a fortune manufacturing plastic eyeglasses and spent most of his money starting and running the Nobel Prize Sperm Bank.

geniuspermbank.com

Graham believed the human race was getting dumber over time and that the only way to stop this decline was to have Nobel Prize winners and men with an IQ of 180 donate to the sperm bank.

Charles Lindbergh was also a believer in eugenics and wanted to populate the world with superior children. He had done so in the 1960s when he had fathered four children, three by two sisters and another by a woman living in Germany. Lindberg had also contributed to the Sperm Bank.

mnhs.org/lindbergh/learn/family/double-life

Pearl wasn't able to conceive a child. She went to her brother's sperm bank and asked for help. Nine months later, Bobbie was born.

When Bobbie was 14 years old, he asked his mom, "Who's my father?"
Pearl's answer was always the same, "He's a genius."

When Bobbie learned one of the donors to the Genius Sperm Bank was Charles Lindbergh, he became convinced that Lindbergh was his father. He thought to himself: "Look at Lindbergh's nose, I have the Lindbergh nose!"

Pearl's younger brother was Tim LaHaye, an evangelical Christian minister who wrote the book *Left Behind*. LaHaye's book predicted the Rapture—the second coming of Jesus Christ. It sold over 70 million copies, more than Stephen King and John Grisham's books combined.

LaHaye was featured on the cover of *Newsweek* magazine and made over 100 TV appearances. He was often a guest on the show *Hardball with Chris Matthews*. His message was: "Jesus Christ is coming." He was on the Board of Directors of the Moral Majority, and his closest friends were Oliver North and Joseph Coors. Tim often said he was instrumental in helping George Bush get elected to his second term as president of the United States. LaHaye sponsored a NASCAR car and named it "Left Behind." It ran the racing circuit for two years and was often left behind. Many evangelicals prayed for LaHaye's car, but Jesus wasn't interested in winning car races. Winning really didn't matter to LaHaye. He wrote off the NASCAR car as an advertising expense.

www.nascar.com

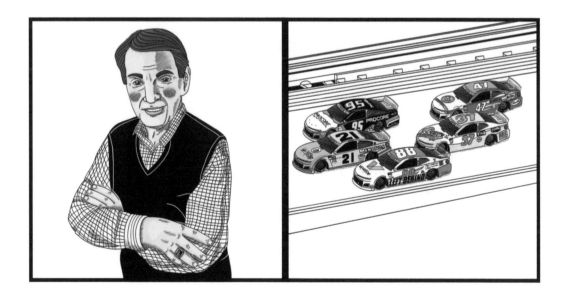

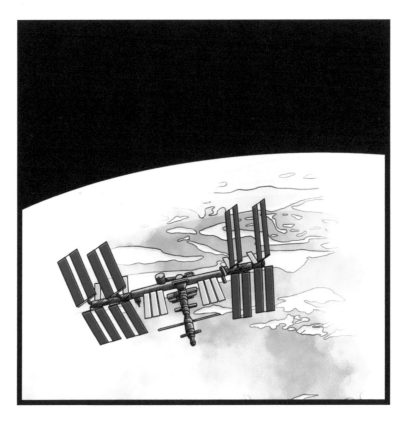

Chapter 9
Cornerstone Television

Tim LaHaye earned over $250 million in royalties from his book *The Rapture*, including the DVD, Audio CD, and movie rights. In under a year, he went on a buying spree for TV stations and media companies:

www.salemmedia.com

$20 million investment in Salem Media Group. (Nasdaq: SALM)

$10 million in Cornerstone Television. Its Sky Angel Satellite reached 100 affiliate stations with an audience of 52 million people throughout the Western Hemisphere.

$20 million invested in infomercials for Don Colbert's book *What Would Jesus Eat Cookbook*. The core buyer of the cookbook was a 44-year-old born again Christian woman, married with three kids living in the American Midwest. In urban areas, the book didn't sell well.

$5 million was invested in TriVita, with $2 million going into promoting one of TriVita's products, Nopalea, a fruit drink made from prickly pear cactus. LaHaye was fined $3.5 million and ordered to pay consumer refunds after the Federal Trade Commission (FTC) court judgment determined that "TriVita and Nopalea didn't reduce swelling of the joints and didn't cure diabetes or skin cancer as claimed." Both products are still available on Amazon for $29.95. The medical community considers the inflammation supplement TriVita and Nopalea to be worthless.

www.consumer.ftc.gov/blog/2014/07/juice-prickly-claims

$5 million investment in Vital Basics Omega fish oil pills. After hundreds of people complained to the FTC, LaHaye had to stop selling Omega Fish Oil. He paid a $2 million fine and was required to refund millions for the false claim that Omega Fish Oil stopped memory loss.

www.trivita.com

LaHaye invested $250,000 in the Christian Vegetarian Association (CVA). It promoted a dietary choice as a way to bear witness to Christ's ministry of love, peace, mercy, and compassion. They believed that a vegetarian diet prepares one for the Peaceable Kingdom, as foretold in the Bible. The food was similar to Jenny Craig's program but without meat.

christianveg.org

LaHaye's investments had put him on the verge of bankruptcy. He decided to unload Cornerstone, and the ideal person to buy it was his sister, Pearl. She was, after all, worth $400 million. He convinced Pearl the best way to promote Bobbie's evangelist career was to own Cornerstone TV.

The network would give Bobbie a path to become an evangelist like Pat Robinson. Bobbie could develop an empire similar to the 700 Club and get listed on the New York Stock Exchange. He could become a Christian media mogul and deliver the message of the Rapture and that the end was near.

www1.cbn.com

LaHaye's pitch to Pearl to buy the Cornerstone Station included the following selling points.

- There are 330,000 churches in America.

- 84% of Americans are Christians.

- 50% of all Americans watch Christian TV programs each month.

- 19% of Americans watch CNN, 18% Oxygen, 16% the Church Channel, 15% VH1 Soul, 13% SoapNet, 11% Golf Channel and 8% MTV.

- The Church Channel had healthy ratings based on millions of visitors and was traded on the NYSE.

- Globally, TV evangelism is a $12 billion industry.

Money wasn't a problem as Cornerstone's sale price was only 7% of Pearl's net worth. She had inherited 90% of the Kirby Vacuum fortune. Two months later, Bobbie was president of Cornerstone Television.

Chapter 10
The Two Headed Turtle

At age 15, Bobbie suffered from *ithyphallophobia* fear of having an erection. He felt like a two-headed turtle. The "good head" fought off evil, while the "bad head" would rise and want the ways of the flesh. The bad head always won, and Bobbie had eight to 10 erections daily.

Bobbie would ask himself, "Should I attend church or stay home and masturbate." He would masturbate and then go to church. If Bobbie looked at a choir girl, he would get a hard-on. His ithyphallophobia was a serious problem.

Bobbie's daily routine was always the same. He would come home from school, go to his room, drop his pants, and lie on his bed. He held his Marilyn Monroe calendar in his right hand, and using his left hand, he masturbated. He used the *Reader's Digest* to catch the sperm between its pages. The trick was not to overshoot the Digest and let the sperm land on his t-shirt.

www.fearof.net/fear-of-an-erect-penis-phobia-ithyphallophobia-or-phallophobia/

Pearl was happy that Bobbie was spending hours in his bedroom with copies of the *Reader's Digest* and *LIFE* magazine. She did not know that under his mattress was a January 1955 Marilyn Monroe Calendar.

marilynmonroe.ca/camera/calendar/index.html

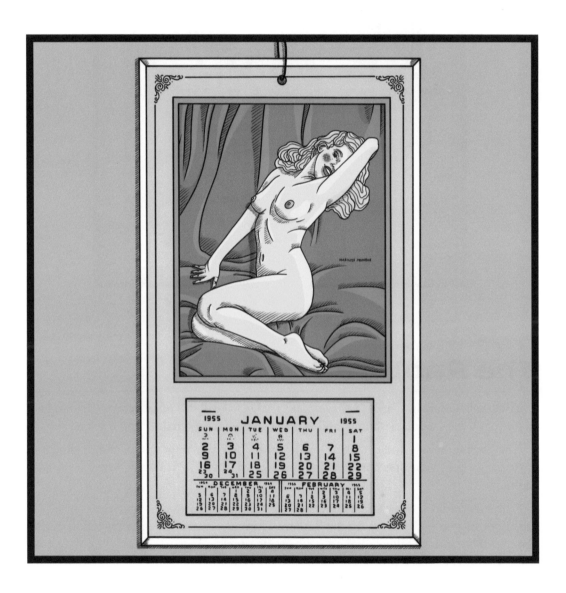

Chapter 11

The Rapture

All true believers in Christ *(1 Corinthians 15:51-58)* will disappear, leaving behind just a pile of clothes, eyeglasses, rings, and watches as they ascend naked into heaven.

The Rapture Ready Index is the Dow Jones Industrial average of the end of time activity. It's a prophetic speedometer that had maxed out at 225. Bobbie knew Jesus was coming.

Christian radio minister Harold Camping told his followers to quit their jobs, sell their possessions and prepare for the Rapture. Using the money given by his followers, he bought thousands of billboards across the nation proclaiming:

Judgment Day - May 21

On the much anticipated Judgment Day, nothing happened. So Harold then simply moved the Rapture date to October 21. When the world didn't end, Harold pledged to quit prophesying it.

After Camping's Rapture predictions failed, Bobbie stopped listening to his radio broadcasts. He started reading weekly apocalypse gauge *The Dead Frog Report, (Rev 3:11.)* "Behold, I come quickly."

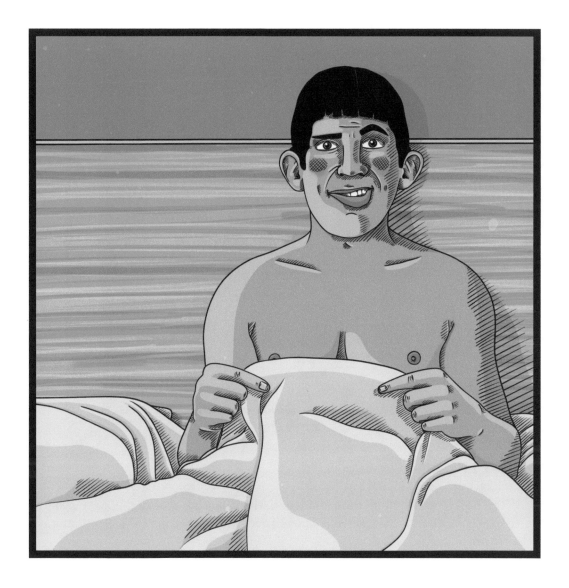

It was Saturday morning. Bobbie was lying in bed playing with his penis and watching a Popeye cartoon. Suddenly he had a vision that "he alone" would create the Rapture by releasing Anthrax at Disney World speeding up Uncle Tim LaHaye's prophecy of the Rapture. Bobbie had faith that Jesus would fulfill his prophecy, descend to Earth and "In the twinkling of an eye, at the last trumpet," create the Rapture.

www.raptureready.com

Chapter 12
L'Abri

When Bobbie turned 17, Pearl sent him to L'Abri (French for "Shelter"), an evangelical Christian community in Switzerland. It was basically a large chalet for the curious travelers to discuss religious beliefs.

labri.org

Bobbie was now hanging out with the sons of Oral Roberts, Robert A. Schuller of Crystal Cathedral fame, and Randy Ross, whose parents owned the Ross Bicycle Company. Randy was buddies with the country singer Billy Ray Cyrus. Both young men enjoyed smoking weed. When they offered Bobbie a drag, he declined. Bobbie spent hours discussing the *Turner Diaries*. The book had a big influence on his thinking about the Rapture.

Jimmy Swaggart, a gospel singer and Pentecostal minister, was the most watched televangelist in the nation. His ministry was generating over 100 million dollars a year when he was caught with a prostitute.

He announced his resignation from the Assembly of God Church which said it was defrocking him for rejecting punishment it had ordered for "moral failure." Weeks later he showed up at L'Abri in Switzerland. Jimmy hung out for three days and then disappeared.

Bobbie soon heard that Swaggart was in the physical therapy room waiting for a massage. When the therapist entered the room, Swaggart was standing there naked with an erection. He asked her to touch his penis, and she refused. He began to masturbate, and his sperm shot into the air and landed on her white shoes. She swore at Swaggart and threatened to report the incident to L'Abri management.

Swaggart began crying and speaking in tongues. He stopped for a minute and, in an angry voice, said to her. "If you tell anyone about this, God will punish you."

Bobbie wondered about the sexual behavior of evangelical ministers. First, he searched Wikipedia under the heading "Sexual misconduct of evangelical preachers." Then he Googled the phrase, "Sexual behavior of Evangelical ministers."

Pat Robertson: Founder of CBN, Christian Broadcasting Network. Pat was a media mogul who ran for president of the United States. He founded the 700 Club and often suggested that women should provide a better home so "the man" doesn't wander. He had a law degree from Yale University but failed the bar exam. He divorced his wife after she developed Alzheimer's.

Robinson's net worth is $100 million.

patrobinson.com

Peter Popoff: A debunked clairvoyant and faith healer. Popoff was exposed for using a concealed earpiece to receive messages from his wife. He went bankrupt and came back with Miracle Spring Water. When asked about sex, Peter said he only enjoyed sex in the missionary position.

Net worth was $23 million.

peterpopoff.com

Kenneth Copeland: A man of God who founded the Kenneth Copeland ministries. He is an author, a public speaker, and a musician. Ken is said to be the richest pastor in the world. His flamboyant lifestyle included three private jets that he used for trips to resorts, personal vacations, and his ministry. Some seven million people listen and view his sermons. Bobbie wondered if Kenneth was ready for the Rapture.

Copeland's annual income exceeds $500,000,000.

www.kcm.org

Joyce Meyer: According to Wikipedia, she was sexually abused by her father. Her first husband had many affairs and convinced her to steal payroll checks from her employer so they could vacation in California.

Net worth $9.5 million

www.joycemeyer.org

Joel Osteen: Joel is an American preacher, televangelist, and author who has a net worth estimated at $100 million dollars. He is considered one of the wealthiest and most popular preachers in the USA. He is currently under fire for leading a luxurious lifestyle. Bobbie couldn't, on Google, find any information on Osteen's sex life. He did learn that Osteen spent $36,300 on a facelift that included an eyelid tuck.

His net worth is $100 millon.

www.joelosteen.com

Jimmy Bakker & Tammy Bakker: Jim got caught with Jessica Hahn, who wasn't his wife. Jim and Tammy hosted the PTL Club and developed Heritage USA, a now-defunct theme park. He was convicted of fraud and spent two years in prison.

Their net worth $500,000.

www.biography.com/news/tammy-faye-jim-bakker-relationship-scandals

Robert Tilton: He was considered the most charismatic and eccentric minister on TV. His Success-N-Life program was aired via 1,400 satellite stations and made millions of dollars. He would preach, "I want to see a $1,000 vow of faith. The bigger the gift, the better the miracle."

The $149.99 Red Prayer Cloth programs generated one million dollars per month. Robert Tilton had also exposed himself at L'Abri. Afterward, he was banned from the community.

His net worth was $120 million.

successnlife.com/

Benny Hinn: He was romantically involved with Paula White, another TV preacher. She had made millions selling the CD set "Creating Healthy Relationships." Hinn's wife learned about Benny's affair with Paula and divorced him.

His net worth is $60 million.

www.bennyhinn.org

Ravi Zacharias: Ravi would expose himself at the spas he owned and masturbate during treatment. He was constantly asking women to have sex with him. A Canadian woman who went public inspired other victims to come forward, and together they sued him for millions. He was, however, protected from judgments for many years by non-disclosure agreements that had been signed by most of the women.

His net worth is $8 million.

rzim.org

John Hagee: John Hagee believed that any woman who shouts out the name of God during sex should be killed.

His net worth is $5 million.

www.jhm.org

Ted Haggard: He picked up a prostitute in New Orleans who then refused to give him a blow job for $10. Ted ended up paying her $20 to just watch him masturbate. He was later outed by a male prostitute Mike Jones (not the songwriter). Haggard was forced to resign as president of the National Association of Evangelicals and was fired from his New Life Church.

His net worth is $200,000.

en.wikipedia.org/wiki/Ted_Haggard

Jerry Falwell Jr.: A business partner revealed he had years-long sex relationships with both Becki and Jerry Falwell. Falwell was forced to resign from Liberty University when a photo of him on a yacht with a young woman was published (both wearing pants that were unzipped.) Liberty University sued Falwell for $40 million in damages for breach of contract and violation of fiduciary duty. The suit was dropped because Falwell's entanglement with the school's finances would jeopardize Liberty's tax-exempt status. Liberty paid Falwell $20 million in severance.

His net worth is $200 million.

en.wikipedia.org/wiki/Jerry_Falwell_Jr.

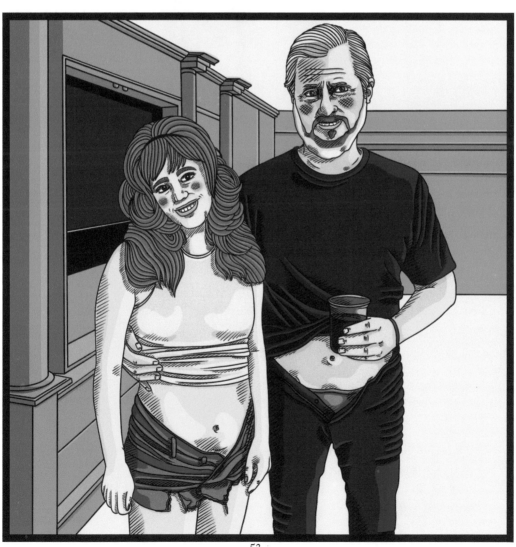

Chapter 13

The Green Prayer Handkerchief

Don Stewart was a faith healer. He'd hold up his trademark green handkerchief, look into the TV camera and plead. "Pray into the green handkerchief! Send it back to us with your donation to the Don Stewart Association. We'll place the handkerchief in the prayer chest. Within three days, all of your prayers will be answered! I will pray and use my God-given healing powers to cure all your ailments, give you abundant blessings and financial prosperity."

The handkerchief crusade was so successful that it had several copycats, including Robert Tilton's own handkerchief program. He called it the "Red Prayer Cloth."

Tilton would tell his TV viewers to write their name, current date, and the time of day on a red cloth. Next, they were told to place the cloth under their pillow and allow God's spirit to work while sleeping. In the morning, they remove the Red Cloth from under their pillow, touch it to their heart, forehead, and pocketbook and then make a $100 donation to: *Robert Tilton, Box 22066, Tulsa, OK 74121*

donstewartassociations.com/prayer_cloth.html

The Church Channel carried Tilton's Red Cloth Prayer programming to 128 million viewers. It was three times larger than Don Stewart's Green Handkerchief program, and it raked in $1 million a month.

The Federal Trade Commission (FTC) filed a deceptive practices suit against Don Stewart and Robert Tilton. They claimed the handkerchief programming was an advertisement because they asked for money in exchange for prayers being answered. The judgment stated that Don Stewart and Robert Tilton could not prove that anyone's prayers had ever been answered. The FTC fined each organization two million dollars. Tilton and Stewart were also banned by the Better Business Bureau.

www.bbb.org

"Judgment Day May 21, 2001 ... Cry Mightily Unto God Jonah 3:8 The Bible Guarantees It!"

www.familyradio.org

On the Trinity Foundation website, Bobbie discovered the information about the Green Handkerchief and Red Prayer Cloth Scams and other "dirt" about the evangelical community. All you need to be an evangelical minister is belong to the Salem Media group or own a TV satellite.

He filled out one 3x5 card for each pastor.

- Jimmy Swaggart: Caught with prostitute and masturbation in public
- Pat Robertson: Divorced his wife when she got cancer
- Peter Popoff,: Ministry went bankrupt
- Benny Hinn: Cheated on his wife with another pastor's wife
- Tammy Bakker and Jim Bakker: Convicted of fraud
- Robert Tilton: Red Cloth scam
- Don Stewart: Green Handkerchief scam
- Ravi Zacharias: Masturbation in public
- Ted Haggard: Caught with a prostitute, twice.
- Robert Schuller: Crystal Palace bankrupt.
- Joyce Meyer: Stole company payroll
- Jerry Falwell Jr.: Sex with a young woman, not his wife
- Kenneth Copeland: Lavish lifestyle with numerous homes and three luxury private jets.

trinityfoundation.org

Bobbie looked at his list of evangelicals and realized they all had gained personal wealth from the hands of everyday people. The evangelical pastors and ministers all lived lavish lifestyles with million-dollar homes with swimming pools and Lear jets.

Then after Bobbie's Uncle LaHaye paid a $3.5 million refund to consumers for the deceptive claim that Cactus Juice cured diseases, he no longer believed in the Rapture and that only 144,000 people would join Jesus in heaven.

Bobbie's anger grew to a point where he decided to destroy the evangelical community and knew the Conference of Evangelical Ministers (SCEM) would soon hold its annual conference at the West Lake Resort in Orlando, Florida. His plan was to release the anthrax virus at Disney World, and if the winds were blowing in the right direction, the virus would infect the West Lake Resort in about an hour.

Chapter 14
Pumpkinville, SC

Bobbie spent a year in Switzerland and returned to America to enroll at Bob Jones University in Greenville, NC. His first year did not go well. A female student he had been dating went to the school's counseling service and filed a complaint. Bobbie apparently was kissing her, and when he reached up under her blouse, he'd managed to unhook her bra and tried to touch her breast.

To settle the misconduct claim, the university paid the woman $10,000. All records of the "Bobbie event" were purged.

This was not the first sexual misconduct claim filed against a male student at BJU. Many male students thought BJU stood for "blow job university." The university had a legal team on retainer with money set aside for such events. The drop-out rate for female students was 60%, with most returning to the safety of their Christian homes. Most now work at Starbucks.

Two years later, Bob Jones University issued Bobbie a certificate stating he was an ordained Christian minister. That same year his mother made a second $50,000 donation to the school.

Bobbie's first ministry was at Soapstone Church in Pickens, South Carolina. The town, located on the Blue Ridge Parkway, is known for hosting the Pumpkintown Festival featuring several U-pick patches, a giant pumpkin contest, and photos in the Pumpkin Chariot. The Perkins Chamber of Commerce boasted the Pumpkintown Mountain Opera. It was a family-friendly daytime event that held an off-color version of the show at 8 p.m. on weekend nights.

On Friday night, over 150 people came to the church fish-fry and, on Sundays, attended church to hear Bobbie preach. He'd speak with rage about feminists, Hollywood elites, and "NPR liberals" who read The New York Times. Bobbie was anti-evolution, anti-Freud, anti-Catholic and anti-feminist. He preached that the Harry Potter books were the devil's work, claiming they promoted witchcraft and would destroy the moral fabric of society.

When Disney World supported "Gay Days," Bobbie proclaimed, "I want to destroy Disney World. I will take out Disney World and the Evangelical Convention with Anthrax at the same time."

Chapter 15
Girls Gone Wild

One evening Bobbie's "two-headed turtle" again raised its ugly head. He asked one of the choir girls over to his house to watch Mel Gibson's *The Passion of Christ*. To his surprise, she accepted his invitation. So that afternoon, to calm his nerves, he masturbated twice. She arrived as planned at his apartment early Saturday night.

They were seated on the sofa in front of the TV when Bobbie pressed play on the VCR, and much to his surprise, a *Girls Gone Wild* tape began playing. The young woman fled the apartment.

Bobbie was forced to resign from the church and left for Boston. There he landed a job as the Assistant Minister at First Church of Christ in Marblehead, Massachusetts.

Bobbie rented a luxury apartment near Salem. One evening he was walking the North Shore Mall and came across a Bikram Yoga studio. As he watched the women hold numerous poses, his two-headed turtle woke up. He signed up for a yoga class.

Bobbie arrived early for his first class, placing his yoga mat at the back of the room. From this location, he had the best view of women in the downward-facing dog position.

Bobbie wore baggy gym pants leaving room for his erections. Bobbie knew he would be hitting *Reader's Digest* real hard after class. Bobbie thought maybe he was addicted to sex and wondered if he got erections while sleeping.

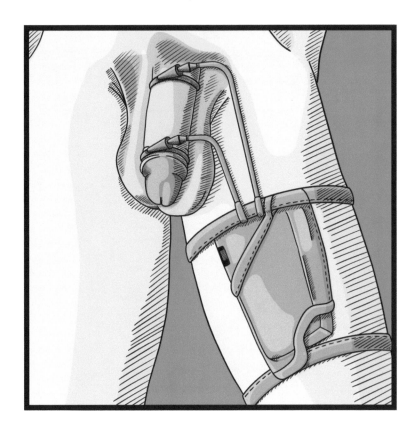

On the internet, he found the Nocturnal Penile Tumescence (NPT) testing device. Using PayPal, Bobbie bought it from the International Society for Sexual Medicine for $49.99.

The NPT device involved placing two bands around his penis and connecting them to the RigiScan® monitor. That night the NPT device recorded nine erections.

Bobbie didn't like the straps holding his penis, so he put the NPT into a Ziploc bag and tossed it in the garbage.

Bobbie went to Google and found an article describing the medical condition known as priapism. It affects 28 percent of Tour de France riders and is brought on by a bicycle seat bouncing against the base of the penis, which pushes up against the prostate gland causing a full erection.

This type of erection could last for hours, making wives and some girlfriends very happy. Bobbie didn't ride a bicycle and knew his erections were natural.

On Wikipedia, Bobbie found instructions for a tumescence test using postage stamps. He purchased the stamps from the Post Office, and that night he carefully wrapped the stamps around his penis. And, sure enough, in the morning, the roll was broken, adding more proof that he was having nighttime erections.

en.wikipedia.org/wiki/Nocturnal_penile_tumescence

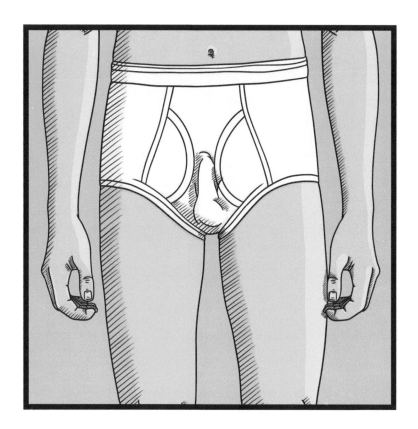

Chapter 16
J.C. Penney

Bobbie had lived in Marblehead for a few months when he developed a new phobia: gephyrophobia, the fear of bridges.

en.wikipedia.org/wiki/Gephyrophobia

When he drove across the Tobin bridge, the metal grating roadway caused the car tires to hum. The sensation gave him a super hard-on, causing him to ejaculate into his underwear.

Driving across the bridge was terrifying and yet oddly satisfying. When he came, he would take the first off-ramp and stop at McDonald's. He used the Men's room to clean up and tossed the soiled underwear in the trash bin.

The McDonald's janitorial staff found the soiled underwear and reported it to management. Bobbie always carried extra pairs of underwear in the glove compartment of his car. He never knew when he would encounter another bridge with a metal grating.

www.jcpenney.com/m/company-info

THE DEAD FROG REPORT

- Most US manufacturing is outsourced to China.

- Gambling is legalized in almost every state.

- People killing each other over minor conflicts.

- The deer population exploded in the New England states.

- Individuals commit crimes and show no remorse.

- Prostitutes would become nuns overnight. (The Dead Frog Report was unable to verify this was currently happening, but the reporter made a note to himself to interview a few nuns.)

- Doctors help the sick kill themselves.

- An increasing number of gay characters appearing on TV.

- Christian networks replacing their gospel programs with infomercials.

- Weather disasters as signs that the second coming is approaching.

- Ads for condoms promoting immoral acts.

(Note: The Frog report was recently removed from the internet.)

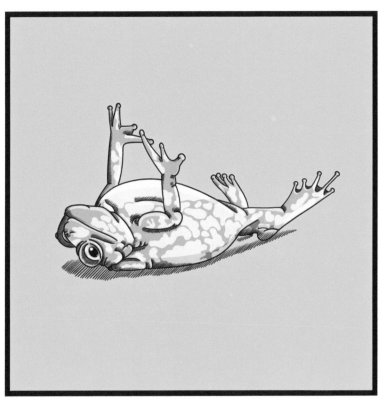

Chapter 17

Institute of Molecular Genetics

Bobbie googled "anthrax" and felt like he'd won the lottery when 23,690,000 links came up. He found 2,695 books dealing with anthrax on Amazon. This number is also Trader Joe's product code for the soft pre-baked baguette.

Bobbie used a VPN to mask his IP address to buy anthrax. He then used Tor and searched Silk Road 2.0. It had hundreds of links to website sites selling drugs and weapons.

www.torproject.org

Then he found the website for the Institute of Molecular Genetics in Moscow, Russia. They would sell to the "right buyer" small quantities of anthrax, botulism, smallpox, and ebola. He e-mailed the Institute to ask about the process to buy anthrax.

The following morning he received an e-mail response from Institute representative Dr. Bob Benthall. He told Bobbie that in order to gain access to the Institute website, he would need to create a fake identity.

www.mcb.nsc.ru

Bobbie used his Bank of Boston VISA credit card and bought an identity package. It included a new Social Security card, a State of Massachusetts driver's license, and a US passport. The total cost was $1,260 dollars.

Name: Bobbie Jones
Address: P.O. Box 202
City, State: Cambridge, MA
Zip: 01915
Phone: 401-783-7770
Occupation: VP, Edison Light Bulb Co.
SS #: 549-849-0660
Marital Status: Single
Mother's Maiden Name: LaMonde
Checking account: Bank of Boston, routing 112004479, acct. 5391041122
Credit Card: Visa 4039-2722-6662-1722, Exp. 04/06
Birthplace: Quincy, Massachusetts
Date of Birth: February 22, 1972
Gender: Male
Highest Educational Level: Ph.D. Chemistry Oxford, Univ. U.K.
Driver's license: F03711761
Passport number: 606845568 Exp. 04/2011
Vehicle ID: 12-584-486840230548234950
AOL password: Rapture2202

Three weeks later, his new identity arrived at his Kinko's post office box. As instructed, he again contacted Dr. Benthall to buy 453.592 grams (one pound) of Anthrax. What Bobbie didn't know was that he was about to buy military-grade Anthrax-836.

Two weeks later, Bobbie received an invoice for $25,000. As instructed, he used Silk Road 2.0 and transferred the money using Cryptocurrency to Defcon Industries, Bank of St. Petersburg, Russia.

Dr. Benthall wasn't a doctor but a retired Russian military colonel, working out of his Moscow apartment. He received the password "ZHOPA1" along with a link to a secure page on the High Molecular Institute website hours after making the Cryptocurrency payment. He was given a 12-hour window to purchase the anthrax. They also offered him a small amount of Novichok.

Bellingcat, a Netherlands-based investigative journalism website that specializes in fact checking, had published articles exposing Dr. Benthall as being a person who pretends to be a Russian Army agent to sell weapons and drugs on the internet.

www.bellingcat.com

He'd made a small fortune selling anthrax, plague, and other biochemical materials to Kim Jong-il of North Korea and Saudi Arabian King Faisal.

Dr. Benthall e-mailed Bobbie to tell him that the anthrax strain he'd purchased had been tested on a donkey. The animal had a seizure and immediately died. He asked Bobbie if he wanted to see a photo of the dead donkey. Bobbie declined the offer.

Benthall also informed him the anthrax he'd purchased had the military code of 2202. This number was cross-checked with the Biopreparat Lab handbook. The day before he left for Russia, Bobbie received an e-mail from Benthall saying,

"We can offer you a stinger missile for $900."

Chapter 18
Blenko Glass

Pearl could see the stress on Bobbie's face. He was not enjoying being the director of Cornerstone Television. She suggested he get married.

Bobbie googled "how-to-buy a bride" and found they were available from $12,000 to $35,000. He looked at available young women from Russia, Ukraine, and Asia. The prices for a younger bride was, of course, higher.

russianbrides.com

Bobbie decided it would make sense to travel to Moscow and pick up the anthrax.

He could at the same time meet some Russian girls and maybe his bride. She would have to be Christian and a student of Bikram Yoga.

Bobbie filled out the questionnaire on a Russian Brides' website and was careful not to mention his ithyphallophobia affliction. The five-day trip, including a first-class hotel, would cost $13,800.

In order to cover travel expenses, Bobbie went on eBay and posted a 1611 King James Bible for sale. He listed the starting price at $10,000. It quickly bid up to and sold for $25,367. His PayPal account sent a notice that the money had been deposited in the Bank of Boston.

Bobbie liked to purchase rare books from local thrift shops and bookstores and then resell them at a huge markup on eBay, Alibris, and Abe Books. Grieving offspring dealing with their parent's estates didn't grasp the value of what books they had, and Bobbie was happy to take advantage of them.

If Bobbie needed more money, he could always borrow some from Pearl. After all, she had a $15,000 monthly allowance from the Kirby Vacuum Cleaner Trust.

Her great-grandfather developed and patented the suction valve for the electric vacuum cleaner. In the 1930s, he sold the patent to the Kirby Vacuum Cleaner, and now the family trust took care of Pearl, her brothers, and several distant cousins.

Pearl collected art by Cape Ann artists Fitz Hugh Lane and Winslow Homer. She also owned several paintings by the California artist Thomas Kinkade.

Her specialty was collectible glass, and she prided herself on owning numerous Blaschka and Chihuly pieces. She also loved the Blenko glass works and engaged in bidding wars to buy his works on eBay.

blenko.com

Chapter 19

Dr. Benthall

Bobbie and Dr. Benthall agreed to meet at the Café Coffeemania in Moscow. They would find each other based on their hats. Bobbie would wear his Boston Red Sox baseball cap and Bentall a classic Russian fur cap with ear flaps.

Once the introduction was made, they moved to a small table. Benthall handed Bobbie a small shoebox containing what looked like a Starbucks sugar bottle. Bobbie handed Benthall a large insulated Trader Joe's shopping bag stuffed with cash. The meeting took less than 20 minutes.

Closing this deal was crucial for Dr. Benthall as he was due to make a final payment on an apartment building in Istanbul, Turkey.

coffeemania.ru/

Chapter 20
Doggie Down

That evening Bobbie went to the dance club Night Flight, where he met girls from Russia, Kazakhstan, and Uzbekistan. Most spoke a heavily accented English.

When Bobbie met Helga, a blond, short Russian girl, he knew that she was the one. She spoke excellent English and told Bobbie she was an instructor at Moscow's Bikram Yoga school. After just one drink, she agreed to have sex for $100. Once they left the club, the big bad turtle raised its head.

They made small talk while getting undressed. Bobbie asked Helga if they could have sex while she was in the Yoganidrasana position. She said she would try, but sometimes she couldn't get her left leg behind her head.

en.wikipedia.org/wiki/Bikram_Yoga

On the bed in his hotel room, Bobbie gently pushed her left leg up and was able to get it behind her head. She was now ready. He gently pushed his penis inside what he considered was heaven. He pumped twice and climaxed.

Now Bobbie asked for a blowjob. Helga said the $100 agreement was for sex and didn't include a blowjob. She agreed to have sex for a second time in the Downward Facing Dog position. Bobbie gave her a quick thumping climaxing in just five strokes.

Bobbie now wanted to have sex for the third time. Helga resisted saying, "Wait until I get to Boston. I can do deep throat." Bobbie replied excitedly, "I have the Deep Throat VCR tape!"

She stuck out her tongue rolled it into a tube shape, thrusting it back and forth, something that only 20% of the people of European ancestry can do. Oh my God! Bobbie thought to himself, Helga can do Downward Facing Dog and roll her tongue! What more could a man ask for?

en.wikipedia.org/wiki/Tongue_rolling

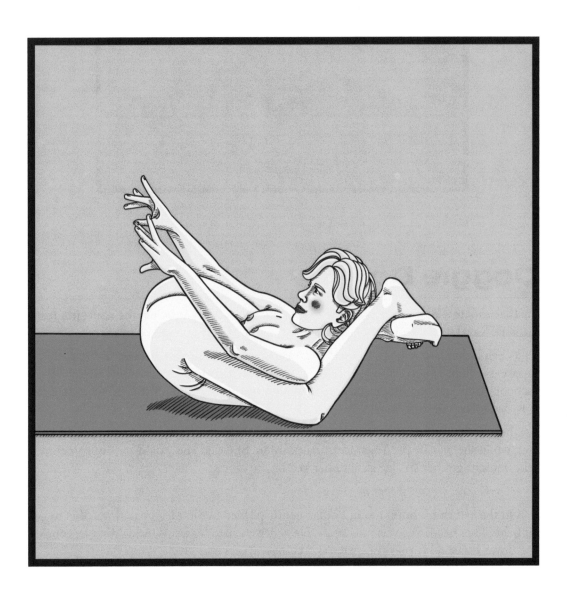

Chapter 21

Christian with a Credit Card

Helga loved sex. She'd lost her virginity at age 15 and had sex with numerous men and boys. Some paid, and some didn't, depending on her mood. Tall men always paid more because they had more money.

Helga was not religious, but she agreed to convert to Christianity before leaving Bobbie's hotel room. They got down on their knees and placed their arms on the edge of the bed.

Bobbie asked her to close her eyes and to repeat after him, "I accept Jesus Christ as my personal savior" (*John: 3:16*). She repeated the words and was now a Christian. He gave her $3,500 in cash and a Wells Fargo credit card with a $5,000 limit.

The following day Bobbie packed his backpack for the flight to Boston. He slipped the NOFI bottle into a gym sock and placed it inside a Nike shoe. Bobbie wondered if one pound of Anthrax was enough to kill everyone on earth.

Chapter 22
The Nesting Dolls

Bobbie looked like a typical American tourist in his Boston Red Sox Jacket. He cleared customs in London and again at Logan in Boston. After all, Bobbie's passport claimed he was the vice president of Edison Light Bulb Company.

Back in Boston, he told Pearl the wonderful news. He'd met a young Russian girl. She was a Christian, and they talked about marriage. He didn't mention she was a Bikram Yoga instructor because he was sure Pearl thought yoga was an Asian religion.

Bobbie gave Pearl a set of Russian Babushka Nesting Dolls that he purchased at the Sheremetyevo Pushkin International Airport gift shop. Neither Pearl nor Bobbie noticed that the dolls were made in China.

Every year Kirby Vacuums gave Bobbie the newest top-of-the-line vacuum cleaner. He had it shipped to Helga. She wouldn't know it was made in China.

www.kirby.com

The following week a woman at Russian Romance tours in Boston helped Bobbie file the K-1 petition for his fiancée to come to America. The 12-step petition took three months to complete.

1. File the 1-129 form Petition with the USCIS.

2. Once the petition is received, a notification is sent.

3. When the petition has been approved Notice of Action (NOA2) is sent.

4. The case goes to National Visa Center, which will handle the K-1.

5. Then the case moves to the U.S. Embassy (Expect to wait four weeks)

6. U.S. Embassy sends your fiancé a package to complete the paperwork.

7. Fiancé gathers documents for the embassy.

8. Medical exam ensues.

9. Embassy interview is given. Bring your passport.

10. K-1, Helga's visa is issued.

11. Helga enters the U.S.

12. The wedding must occur within 90 days.

The "alien" must file an adjustment of statute petition to receive a green card. Bobbie thought to himself that Helga's visa application was more difficult than buying Anthrax.

Six months later, Helga received the K-1 permission to travel to America. She had a lot to do before leaving Moscow. She needed to update her passport photo, pay off the dance club, pay back a loan from an old boyfriend, and send money to her parents.

Helga bought new dresses at the House of Fashion on Pyatnitskaya Street. She then went to Ooh-La-La, a high-end lingerie boutique, and bought a fancy bra. She went for a pedicure and got her toenails painted a dragon-fire red. Finally, she had her hair permed by her favorite stylist.

Helga was seated in first class on Aeroflot and dressed to the nines for the flight to Boston. She thought to herself: "I look like the American movie star Nicole Kidman."

Chapter 23

Krispy Kreme

One week after arriving in Boston, Helga was in the back seat of Pearl's Lexus, accompanying Pearl and Bobbie to Logan International Airport. Bobbie had a $99 Orlando-bound Southwest flight to catch.

On the way home, Pearl stopped at the drive-through window at a Krispy Kreme. She always bought doughnuts whenever the KKD stock was down. She thought if she purchased a dozen doughnuts, it would be doing her part to help the company turn the corner.

Bobbie was wearing his favorite Red Sox jacket. He was on his mission from God, and today was the day. He was going to Disney World to meet his maker, Jesus Christ.

www.krispykreme.com

Chapter 24
The Fanny Pack

The bottle of NOFI in Bobbie's fanny pack went unnoticed by Logan airport security. He was soon at Terminal B and standing in line at Starbucks. He ordered a Cappuccino Grande, unzipped his fanny pack, and reached in for his wallet. In doing so, he pushed the NOFI bottle up and out of the fanny pack. It hit the concrete floor with a thud and shattered.

The noise caught the barista's attention, who looked at the white powder on the floor and thought someone had dropped a sugar bottle. Bobbie thought he could save the situation and asked the barista for a broom.

She responded, "Starbucks doesn't have cleaning supplies. We use the airport janitorial service." Bobbie then asked the barista for an empty cup so he could clean up the "sugar."

She said, "Sorry, I can't give away coffee cups, but you can buy one for 35 cents."

Bobbie handed her a quarter and a dime.

When the NOFI bottle broke, it created a viral plume containing billions of virus droplets invisible to the human eye.

Bobbie held his breath so as not to inhale the virus and used the side of his shoe to push most of the powder back into the cup. He didn't realize that in doing so, he created another NOFI plume that rose into the air and was sucked up into the Logan Airport ventilation system. Within an hour, NOFI had spread throughout the airport.

The scene that evening at the Boston Logan Airport was eerie. The only sound coming from the terminal was the humming of the moving walkways. Airline passengers collapsed then, and their bodies were carried to the end of the walkway, joining a growing pile. Overhead a voice continued advising, "The moving sidewalk is ending. Please watch your step for human remains."

The largest pile of bones was at the double-wide sidewalk in the Delta terminal.

Chapter 25
The Bombfire

Waiting in line, including Bobbie, were six customers. (1 + 6 = 7). In seven days, as vectors carrying the virus, they killed two billion people.

-Seven is considered a lucky number by gamblers.
-Seven is the month of July.
-The earth was created in seven days.
-7UP is a drink.
-Seven sculptures by Richard Serra are located in Doha, Qatar.
-*The Seven* is an episode of Seinfeld.
- Charles Lindberg had seven children by three women in Germany.
-The international calling code for Russia is 7.
-Seven of Nine is a character in *Star Trek: Voyager*.
-7 is a line on the New York Subway.
-*The Magnificent Seven* and *Seven Samurai* are films.
-*The Seven Pillars of Wisdom* is a book by T.E. Lawrence
-There are seven fundamental types of catastrophe.
 -There are Seven Wonders of the World.
-In seven days, the NOFI virus would kill two billion people

All the Starbucks customers that morning were not lucky as they were exposed to NOFI.

Six Starbucks customers

1. Hollywood movie producer **Brian Grazer** was at the airport to catch an LA-bound first-class flight on United. Grazer stepped into the NOFI powder and created a small plume. He inhaled some spores, but he didn't have immediate symptoms. He had 24 hours to live. Grazer was now a vector, and every breath he exhaled contained tens of thousands of spores.

Later that afternoon, he was in the board room at Universal Studios in a meeting with Ron Howard, Mark Cuban, Tom Hanks, and Dan Brown. The group discussed the movie rights to *The Da Vinci Code*. In three days, four of the five people at the meeting would be dead. Tom Hanks, who drank craft beer at Buffalo Bill's Brewery, Hayward, California, was the lone survivor.

Glazer met with Tom Cruise that evening to discuss the financing of movie projects. Cruise could not know that Glazer was a vector and carrying the NOFI virus. Two days after the meeting, both were dead.

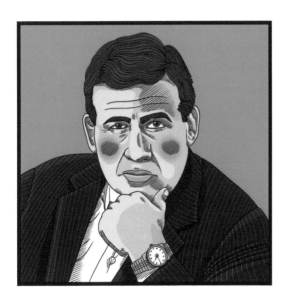

2. TV personality Tucker Carlson's father, **Dick Carlson** was in line at Starbucks and walked through the NOFI spores. He was going to New York City to watch Tucker, who was a contestant on the ABC reality show, *Dancing With the Stars*.

abc.com/shows/dancing-with-the-stars

That morning, Dick Carlson's shoes carried the virus from Boston to NYC exposing his son Tucker Carlson, (1) plus (22) dancers plus (160) people in the audience and (42) ABC staffers.

(1+22+160+42=225)

Order Number 225 is also the parts order number for the gold swan, the faucet on Jimmy Swaggart's jacuzzi. The Antonov AN-225, made in Russia, is the world's largest airplane. The Chicago Electric Welding Stick Welder runs at 225 Amp-AC, 240V. It is also the area code for Baton Rouge, Louisiana. It is a coincidence that 225 has several meanings and that Tucker can't dance.

www.nytimes.com/2002/08/11/magazine/the-odds-of-that.html

3. **Dr. Ken Alibek** was traveling to Washington, D.C. to speak at the Center for Disease Control. The mathematical probability was 120,000,000 to 1 that he would be at Logan Starbucks when Bobbie dropped the NOFI bottle. Alibek heard the thud of a bottle breaking. Like everyone else at Starbucks, he inhaled about 300 spores. He became a walking vector. When he landed in D.C., he took a limo to the Pentagon, where he infected 8,200 people. He then went to the Smithsonian and infected 4,303 people. His last stop was the White House to meet with Vice President Bush and select staff. Passing in the hallway, Senator Mitch McConnell shook Dr. Alibek's hand and told him he was doing a great job protecting American lives.

4. High on Oxycontin and standing in line at Starbucks was **Mike Lindell**, also known as "The Pillow Guy." He looked at the powder on the floor and thought it looked like cocaine. He leaned over, put his index finger into the powder, and rubbed it under his lower lip. In doing so, he ingested over 5,000 spores. Within 30 seconds, he was coughing and fell to the floor, clutching his pillow. He lay there until the paramedics arrived. He was dead when the ambulance reached the hospital.

5. At the end of the Starbucks line was **Rachel Uchitel**, Tiger Wood's girlfriend. She was flying to Miami Beach Club to meet Tiger, and as a vector carrying NOFI, she infected him and all his golfing buddies including the caddies and PGA officials.

www.nytimes.com/2021/08/09/style/rachel-uchitel-tiger-woods-nda.html

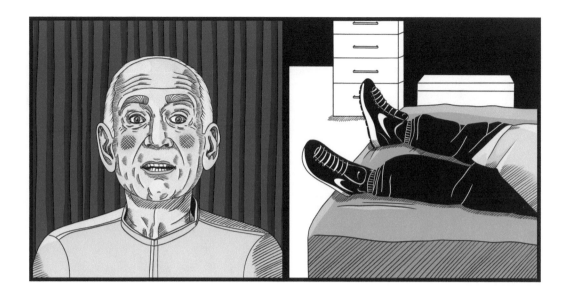

6. At the end of the Starbucks line was **Marshall Applewhite.** He was the leader of the cult *Heaven's Gate.* Marshall was wearing a black shirt, sweat pants, and black Nike Decades athletic shoes. Applewhite and his followers wore Nikes because he got a good deal at Discount Shoes in San Diego.

Applewhite had been in Boston meeting with GEICO insurance representatives. He wanted to buy an Alien Abduction insurance policy for his followers. The meeting went well, and now he was flying to Los Angeles, where he was met by his partner, Bonnie Nettles. She drove him to Rancho Santa Fe for a meeting with his followers. Applewhite had walked through the NOFI virus at Starbucks and, as a vector, carried it to Rancho Santa Fe. The virus killed everyone in the group.

Marshall Applewhite and Ken LaHaye were "truth followers." Both believed the end was near. LaHaye believed the Rapture would occur, taking his followers to heaven. Applewhite and his group were waiting for a spacecraft to take them home to Comet Hale-Bopp.

Chapter 26
Microspores

Bobbie held his breath as he scooped up the NOFI and secured the lid. He still had time to catch his flight to Disney World. He was lucky and had inhaled less than 200 spores. He still had six hours to live.

Every Starbucks customer that day became a human vector and carried the virus on their shoes to all the major airlines: Air Canada, Air France, Alaska, American, Delta, United, and British Airways.

The janitor who came and swept up the remaining NOFI at Starbucks inhaled 3,500 spores and would be dead in an hour. In sweeping up the white powder, he created more plumes of the virus and spread it as he wheeled the garbage can out to the hallway with trash receptacles.

Molinda Palmer was sitting at a table watching Bobbie scoop up the NOFI. She was seated ten feet away from the spill and inhaled enough spores, turning her into a walking vector. She boarded her United Airlines flight to Chicago and was seated in 12-D directly under an air duct. During the flight, her breath containing tens of millions of NOFI micro-spores were sucked into the air and spread throughout the duct system. Within an hour, everyone on the flight was infected with NOFI. Some of the sickest passengers needed wheelchairs to get off the plane.

It was purely happenstance that Molinda would infect 117 passengers on the flight to Chicago. She then attends the Oprah Winfrey Show and sits in the third row. By the end, she had infected 117 people on the Eastern flight, the cab driver, and 280 Oprah audience members.

www.oprah.com

That day in total, she infected 398 people. The number 398 was also on Pliva, the medication that she took for high blood pressure. Pliva will keep her alive for two additional weeks. In this time, she will infect 10,000 more people.

That same afternoon Oprah gave away two hundred and eighty G-6 Pontiac sedans to everyone in the audience. During the videotaping of the show, a few people in the audience got sick and were taken to a local hospital. Most people were able to drive their new Pontiacs home and infect their family and friends.

Oprah and her friend Gayle were the only two survivors from the taping of the "Pontiac" show. The night before the car giveaway show, they ate pizza and drank two (each) Alpha King 12% alcohol beer from the 3 Floyds Brewing. Both women had limousines waiting to drive them home.

Bobbie was now in line at Southwest Gate 22. He approached the boarding gate with his airline ticket between this teeth. In each hand was a Starbucks cup. One held the NOFI virus and the other a cappuccino. He nodded to the gate agent to take the ticket from between his teeth.

She looked at Bobbie holding coffee cups in both hands and wisecracked, "Is that coffee for me"? While the two-headed turtle raised its head, he managed to laugh and reply, "Next time, put your order in early."

In his mind, he thought, "Do downward-facing dog, I'll give you the coffee and my penis!"

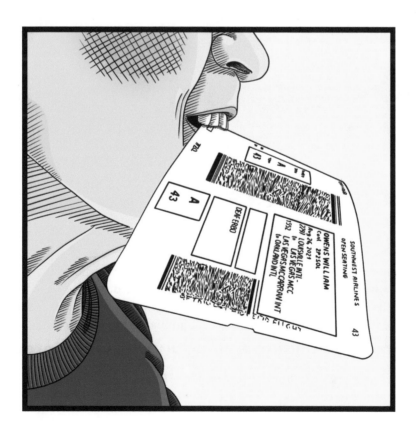

83

Chapter 27
The Architects

The four men seated at a Starbucks table were unaware of the Anthrax spill. They were members of the Architect Institute of America and about to embark on a round-the-world trip photographing and writing about the world's most iconic buildings. The book's working title was *Buildings You Should See Before You Die*. Bobbie had just dropped the bottle of anthrax and, in the clean up process, the spores drifted to the architects' table. They became vectors carrying the anthrax virus around to the world.

The following building and countries were infected

- The Gherkin Building, London, UK. *(Upper Left)* Named the Gherkin because it resembles a gherkin cucumber 41 stories with 7,429 panes of glass the home of SKY-TV.

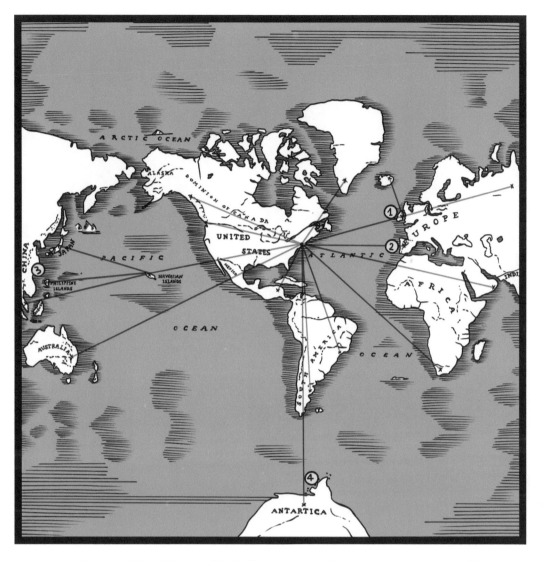

- Petrous Twin Towers, Kuala Lumpur City, Malaysia. *(Upper Right)* The twin towers double-decker skybridge is the highest two-bridge building in the world. In an event of an emergency tenants can be evacuated by crossing the skybridge. The virus took the same route infecting 14,000 people in one day.

- Guggenheim Museum, Bilbao, Spain. *(Lower Left)* the museum has regenerated life in the city of Bilbao. Needless to say the virus killed the staff and visitors from 18 countries.

- City of Shanghai, China. *(Lower Right)* With 26,000,000 people it is the biggest city in China. The architect carrying the NOFI virus infected the entire city. Only about 200,000 beer drinkers survived.

- Antarctica. *(See Chapter 35)* Home to 150,000 emperor penguins.

Chapter 28
Pleasanton, California

In the town of Pleasanton, the traffic signals were working, but there was no traffic. Just off Highway 580 at the Hacienda mini-mall, the Bed Bath & Beyond and Old Navy stores were fully stocked, but no customers came.

The coffee shop at Barnes and Noble Books was open late on Friday night. Saturday morning, the sofa contained piles of bones, as did the adjoining table. Next door, Jamba Juice and Best Buy were closed, and Whole Foods, for the first time, was silent. Across the parking lot, the Regal Theater was playing *The Lord of the Rings*. Theater seats contained the bones of the viewers as the movie played over and over again. The Coke from the fountain was still cold, and the hot buttered popcorn with artificial butter was warm.

Across the freeway from the mini-mall was the Hacienda Business Park. That morning the park sprinklers popped up on the lawn at Allstate, People Soft, and Kaiser Hospital.

On Owens Drive, the big box Walmart sat eerily quiet, its electric doors ready to spring open for customers that didn't come. Friday was always a big shopping day at Walmart. Inside the store, long lines of shopping carts full of merchandise sat at check-out stands. Bones occupied the places people once stood. The virus was especially deadly in closed environments. Getting a burger at McDonald's or a haircut could be a fatal event.

The 24-hour Kinko's and Petco stores were untouched. A few looters had been in Trader Joe's and helped themselves to the entire stock of Two-Buck Chuck, vodka, and frozen pizzas. Some grabbed Semifreddi's sourdough bread, cranberry chèvre, and Toscano cheese. The gourmet, no-fat, high-protein organic granola was left behind.

Cars sat for days at the In-N-Out Burgers drive-through window. Some engines were still idling. A recorded voice broke the silence, "Welcome to In-N-Out Burger. May I take your order?"

At Hooters in Dublin, California, colorful balloons were tied to the front door railing. A sign taped to the door read, "Happy Birthday, Ron." You wouldn't have wanted to look inside. A huge party was going on when the virus hit. The customers were drinking Corona, Miller, and Bud Light, so no one survived. Hooters didn't serve unpasteurized craft beer.

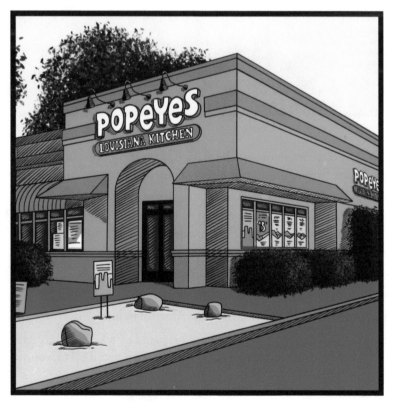

The Dublin Bart train remained at the station, with its doors wide open. Inside, bones were waiting for the forty-minute trip to San Francisco International Airport.

At the Livermore Airport, several small aircraft were parked on the runway waiting to taxi for take-off, but they never moved. One plane had taken off the day before and crashed into nearby suburban homes. The fire department didn't come. Those homes had burned all night.

Hot dogs from Nathan's had quickly disappeared, as did the barbecue ribs at Emil Villa's. Papa John's and KFC were closed as was the Donut-Wheel in Livermore.

The television sets in 380 million homes across America were on...but no one was watching.

Your diet would no longer be based on food prepared by a $7 per hour employee at the Olive Garden, Panera, or Panda Express. If you wanted a green salad, you would have to learn how to grow lettuce.

Chapter 29

Disney World

In two hours and forty minutes, the Southwest Airlines flight had reached Orlando, Florida. Bobbie infected everyone onboard the flight.

1 Bobbie +202 passengers+57,433 Disney Visitors+ 850 Disney staff= 58,486.

It was just a coincidence that the number 58,486 is the population of the city of Oblast where Helga was born.

Bobbie, inside the park, went straight to the Mad Tea Party ride. As the teacups began to spin, he removed the lid from the Starbucks cup. When they seemed at peak speed, he stood up and threw the remaining NOFI into the air. This created a NOFI plume reaching 45-feet in diameter as it drifted out over Disney World. In tossing the NOFI spores into the air, Bobbie inhaled tens of thousands of NOFI spores. He was dead within minutes.

By the end of the day, all the Disney World guests were infected with the NOFI virus. A few people died within three to four hours. Most managed to make it to their hotels.

The next day, of the 500 room at the Disney Hilton, 428 rooms contained bones of NOFI victims. The remaining 72 rooms were occupied by beer drinkers.

Disney World survivors who had spent the day drinking beer at the numerous adult beverage pavilions survived.

Jesus didn't come for Bobbie. The NOFI virus came for Bobbie. He was 27 years old. There is no official "membership" of famous musicians and people who have died at age 27, but now Bobbie had joined the list. Some members of the **"27 Club"** as it has come to be called:

- **Jim Morrison** - Poet, song writer, and lead vocalist of the Doors. Drug overdose. Buried at Père Lachaise Cemetery, Paris, France. Francis Ford Coppola used his music in the film *Apocalypse Now* making Morrison a cult figure.
- **Brian Jones** - Founding member of the Rolling Stones. Death by Drowning.
- **Jimi Hendrix** - Musician. He took barbiturates and asphyxiated on his own vomit in London.
- **Janis Joplin** - Musician. Overdosed on heroin.
- **Ron "Pigpen" McKernan** - Helped form the Grateful Dead. Cirrhosis of the liver from drinking.
- **Peter Ham** - Musician of the band Badfinger, worked with the Beatles, his biggest single was *Come and Get It*. Suicide by Hanging
- **Amy Winehouse** - Musician. Her songs were inspired by drug and alcohol addictions. Died of alcohol poisoning.
- **Kurt Cobain** - Musician. Suicide by gunshot
- **D. Boon** - Musician of the band Minutemen, killed in a van crash.
- **Jean-Michel Basquiat** - Contemporary artist who hung out with Keith Haring and Andy Warhol, "acute mixed drug intoxication."
- **Benjamin Keogh** - Suicide by gunshot. Elvis Presley's grandson and son of Lisa Marie.

www.rollingstorne.comculture-list/the-27-club-a-brief-history.

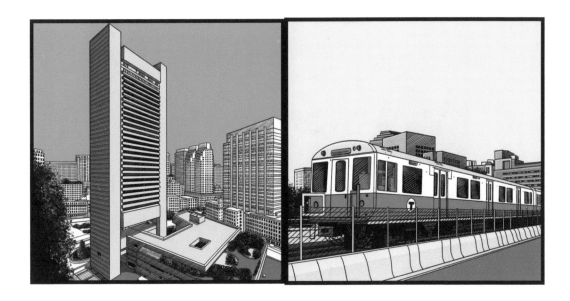

Chapter 30
Bank of Boston

That day the NOFI virus infected the entire city of Boston. People got on the MBTA and couldn't get off. The bodies of dead passengers prevented the train doors from opening and closing.

A senior vice president of the Bank of Boston was picked up by his limo driver at Logan. He carried the NOFI virus on his shoes, delivering it to the high-security board room on the 37th floor.

Ambulances at Logan were the first to respond to the crisis. Then the fire and police departments. Paramedics and EMTs quickly donned white coveralls and bubble suits to protect themselves from the mysterious virus. The first responders noticed that the skin on many victims' hands had turned light blue. Two signs the victim was about to die were a hacking cough and the blueish tinge to the hands due to lack of oxygen.

Later in the afternoon, clothes and bones were scattered around the corporate offices of Bank of Boston. It was a Friday, and many people had left work early to start the weekend. Some carried the virus home to their family. Others delivered it to friends at gyms, bars, and cinemas.

The virus had killed everyone at Mass General in one afternoon. Doctors, nurses, the in-house billing department, janitors, and visiting family all died. NOFI infected the neonatal intensive care unit and killed women waiting to deliver their babies.

The virus even took all the tourists visiting the historical Old Ironside ship and the shoppers at Faneuil Hall Marketplace.

Chapter 31

Russ Limbaugh is Dead

On AM and FM radio stations, Rush Limbaugh confessed that he was addicted to painkillers and let slip his dealer's name.

When the virus infected Limbaugh, he started coughing, and his mouth slipped down on the microphone. It pushed his tongue down his throat, and he choked to death before NOFI did its job. Russ Limbaugh was soon just a pile of bones.

By Friday evening, communication infrastructure across the nation began to fail. First, the AM and FM radio stations stopped broadcasting. Satellite radio played on with pre-programmed music.

NBC, ABC, and CBS went off the air. The independent cable channels ESPN, MTV, CNN, and QVC, continued to broadcast via their own satellites.

Bill O'Reilly began to feel sick while broadcasting *The O'Reilly Factor* on FOX. He threw up on-camera while describing the events across the nation.

Jon Stewart on Comedy Central's *The Daily Show* fared worse. Stewart convulsed and fell to the floor mid-sentence. People thought it was part of his comic routine, but it was real, and he was dead, this time dead as a stone.

On MSNBC's *Hardball*, Chris Matthews showed live video of Times Square. The scene on the streets of New York City was so gruesome that stations cut away to reruns of Mary Poppins.

The Times Square NASDAQ billboard read "Buy Stock Now" then switched to a Lion King commercial. When the commercial ended, the screen changed again, this time showing piles of bones on the Times Square subway platform.

The only people alive were home or in pubs sipping beer and watching CNN and other news channels.

Some tuned in to a Bruce Springsteen interview on *The Larry King Show*. King stopped mid-sentence, looked into the camera, and announced that Donald Trump of NBC's hit show *The Apprentice* was dead. He reported that right after Trump uttered his famous line, "You're fired," he gasped for air, fell over, and died.

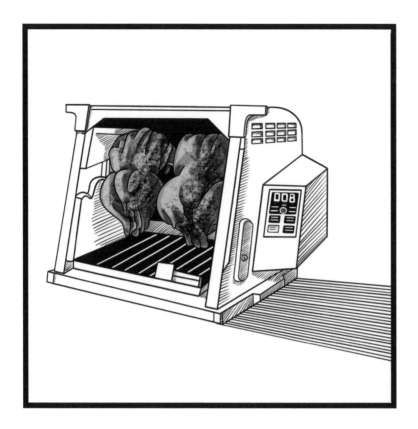

Chapter 32
Set it and Forget It.

In rural Ohio, QVC was running a "Joan Rivers' Stars & Stripes Bee Pins" spot when the virus hit. Station operators knew something was wrong when incoming calls slowed to a trickle. This baffled the staff as credit card orders from the internet were still coming to the QVC Citicorp account at a rate of $15,000 an hour.

TCM was broadcasting reruns of Tony Robbins' *Dare to be Great*. His books, DVDs, and CDs were still selling like hotcakes when the station went off the air. The QVC infomercial for "Ron Popeil Ronco Rotisserie" ran at midnight and 3 AM as scheduled. Unwatched televisions across the nation blared "Set It and Forget It! Kitchen Top Ovens with ONLY Four Easy Credit Card Payments! Call 1-800-946-1133."

www.ronco.com

The "Set It and Forget It" programming stayed on the air for a week while it took NOFI a week to reach the headquarters in Dubai.

Ron's net worth was reported to be over 200 million.

In New York City, the Knicks were playing the Detroit Pistons at Madison Square Garden. Halfway through the game, the entire camera crew for ESPN became deathly ill. The cameras continued broadcasting the deaths of 19,812 basketball fans. The Knicks had died before, but never like this. Another ESPN first!

Bob Dylan was playing Radio City Music Hall. He finished the song "Blowing in the Wind" and left the stage. His bones were found the next day on the steps of the New York City Public Library beneath the Fortitude Lion statue.

C-SPAN broadcasted from the nation's capital. They played a news loop of President Bush's speech from his underground bunker at the White House. After watching Bush, many people wanted to kill themselves as he repeatedly mispronounced the word "Armageddon." It was a sure bet that Bush couldn't spell the word either.

Thousands of Clear Channel radio stations across the nation automatically played Bruce Springsteen's "Born in the USA." *The Howard Stern Show* was about to go off the air when the small wiggly shadowboxes that covered women's breasts disappeared, and you could see pink nipples. Young men everywhere dropped their pants and started masturbating.

www.howardstern.com

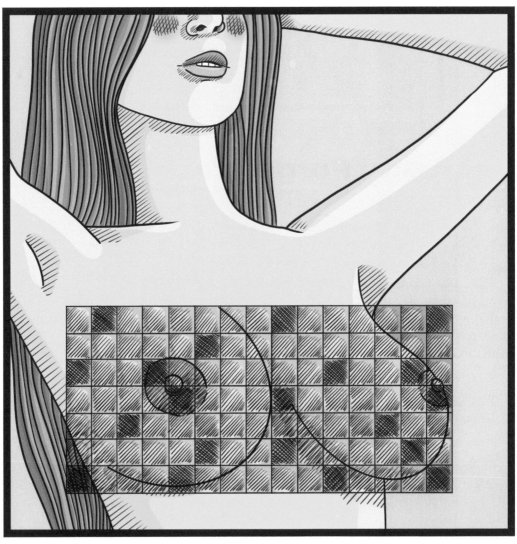

Chapter 33
Dead Penguins

It took NOFI six days to reach Antarctica, where it infected the Swedish research scientists studying the Macaroni Penguin. They all died, including the male Macaroni penguins.

Chapter 34
Jesus Didn't Come

The second coming of Christ didn't occur. Those of us who were left behind were not Evangelical Christians. We were beer drinkers. Unfortunately, Bobbie and Helga were not beer drinkers.

That morning I told the other survivors hanging out at Buffalo Bill's that I was forming a Village with a government patterned after the 12th century Viking governmental system called the *Althing*. I wanted to create a just and efficient society, a decentralized free state in which everyone has voting rights.

Each region (Township) would have an elected leader representative. The only permanent official of the *Althing* was a "lögsögumadr" or law-speaker who had memorized laws and gave advice on governing the regions. The *Althing's* sole purpose would be to settle disputes between individuals and keep government out of the lives of citizens.

I owned the book *Viking Age Iceland* which explained how the government worked, and apparently, that was enough for them.

www.barnesandnoble.com/w/the-viking-age-angus-a-somerville/1134372295

Chapter 35
How to Rebuild Society

The people sitting at Buffalo Bill's weren't concerned about the details of the *Althing* and how a Viking government worked. They trusted me and liked the idea of a community based on townships, little government, individual rights, and bartering for goods.

The problem was: most beer drinkers don't know anything about farming. I was pretty sure that no one sitting at the bar at Buffalo Bill's had ever milked a cow or killed a chicken. Very few could cook, and most people ate at the Olive Garden, Chipotle and Panera.

At the Hayward Library, I found the book *How To Rebuild Civilization* and numerous survival books, including *The Whole Earth Catalogue*. These books, for the most part, are useless because they discuss sustainability as if it was a hobby.

I can assure you that 98% of Americans can't bake bread. Many own a bread baking machine…just add flour, water, and yeast. The books on sustainability show the reader how to operate a sewing machine and ferment a jar of cabbage. The average person can grow tomatoes, lettuce, and carrots in a small raised garden bed. The garden can produce vegetables for a half dozen families for a couple of months. Farmers eat meat and potatoes because they need the calories for good health. Carrots and string beans just don't cut it…

Many survival books give instructions on how to build a log cabin and make soap. People who survived the virus don't want to know how to keep bees or can tomatoes.

I was sure no one at Buffalo Bill's Brewery wanted to read a book or watch a *YouTube* video on how to butcher a steer. I was sure no one drinking beer at Buffalo Bill's Brewery was interested in keeping goats. At the winery, we had wine, a renewable resource. We would barter it for food.

- *The Country Life Handbook*
- *The Medieval Kitchen: Recipes from France and Italy*
- *Bull Cook and Authentic Historical Cooking Methods*
- *Time-Life's Renaissance*
- *Pickled Potted and Canned*
- *The Country Kitchen: a Cooking from Scratch Cookbook*
- *Basic Butchering: Livestock and Game*
- *Guide to Essential Knowledge*
- *Encyclopedia of Natural Medicine*

I was raised on a farm and learned how to take care of chickens. The critical thing about keeping chickens is every night, you have to lock the coop. If you accidentally leave the gate open in the morning, your chickens will be missing or dead. Raccoons and foxes love to kill chickens and eat eggs. If you don't believe me, just leave the door to the chicken coop open.

Eating chickens are called "fryers" and butchered at ten weeks. Let someone else raise the chickens. We'll barter wine for eggs.

Chapter 36
The Pledge

Each new member of the *Althing* community is required to sign the citizenship pledge. We pledged to share the resources (wine & agriculture) of the Livermore Valley. The *Althing* is committed to re-establishing civilization based on the freedoms guaranteed by the former United States of America: Life Liberty and the Pursuit of Happiness. All citizens must contribute to the quality of life in the valley by working and must be trained to handle a deer rifle. All free citizens must also pledge loyalty to the township where they live. Each township Godlord leader, in return, has the responsibility to provide food and shelter to its citizens.

Citizens will be given a wine allotment. They are free to move to any township in the valley he or she chooses. They can barter their wine allotment for additional food, clothing, small animals, or any other goods.

The "lögsögumadr" decides on criminal discipline for any wrongdoing. Punishment may include confiscation of property, food resources, and banishment from the valley. The person banished will be driven to Bakersfield or, worse yet, Los Angeles.

Chapter 37
Citizens of the Althing

Known free thinkers and rugged individualists would not be invited to join our group. Tony and I interviewed everyone who wanted to join the *Althing* community. The questions were simple, and the answers were written on the back of Sam Adams beer coasters.

I asked each person if they knew how to milk a cow. The answer was always "no," But several people did say, "I know how to ski."

Only one person said they had once used jumper cables to start their car. Everyone else answered, "When my car doesn't start, I call AAA." That day eighteen people had signed up to join the Village. Within two months, the community had grown to 42 individuals.

The people who applied were:

- Mitch: 32 years old. At 280 lbs, a loud bartender chef who loves beer and women.

- Joe: 60 years old. A good barber, furniture maker, and general carpenter.

- Gina: Age 36. A well-endowed Sicilian-American. A real handful, she's a waitress who talks non-stop. She owns a sewing machine.

- Stacy: 45 years old. An attorney and workaholic. She loves whiskey. She wants to be the "lögsögumadr" or law speaker, and she can recite the *Althing* laws from memory. She wants to bring her dogs to Livermore.

- Robert: age 45. A roofer, people call him "Tarman." He can fix anything from a dishwasher to a car radio. He sleeps in his van and has a few missing front teeth.

- Dave: 50 years old. Nicknamed "Blockhead." Knows everything about concrete. When not working, he hangs out at the bar, drinking all day.

- Damien: age 56. A Zen master and carpenter. His wife left him ten years ago for another guy. He later learned she was killed when an automated garage door at her apartment building came down on the roof of her car and broke her neck. He's still looking for a soulmate.

- Russ: Age 33. A big talker from New Zealand who loves soccer. He had a wife and a girlfriend. One day his wife went missing. Her body was found floating in the bay near the Dumbarton bridge. He moved back to New Zealand.

- Tony: Age 40. US Army veteran of 82nd airborne with 80 jumps. He has a bad back, a bad knee, and a pinched nerve in his neck. He loves mushrooms, drinking, and women of color.

- Dom: Age 44. Easygoing. An electrician whose hobby is mushroom hunting.

- Jan: Age 50, and Henry age 57. Not married, no kids, they just want a place to stay.

- Victor: Age 50, a house painter who's an alcoholic.

- Jerry; Age 75. Retired government worker. He sits at the bar for hours, reading New Yorker magazine. He'll argue about almost anything.

- Tim: Age 57, wanted to be a poet, but became a salesman peddling insecticides. He loves the smell of roses.

- Rod: Age 50. He is into jewelry and gold sales, some drugs, and is an ex-Christian minister who owns a Harley Davidson. He loves talking about his evangelist grandfather.

- Renee: Age 33. 6' tall, owns a bookstore. She's unmarried with a beautiful free spirit.

- Christy: Age 40. Not married. Another free spirit who enjoys discussing everything. Concerned about the environment, loves to smoke and drinks white wine, lager beers, aged rum, and whiskey.

- April: Age 27. A bartender with long red hair who loves "bad boys." Later became a deputy sheriff. Then married a sheriff, then divorced him.

- Connie: Age 35. Has a candle-making business and developed the candle "This Smells Like My Vagina After Sex." She was ripped off by Gwyneth Paltrow, whose candle was called "This Smells Like My Vagina."

Neither of my ex-wives Janet and Carole or Linda, my girlfriend between the two wives, survived. They all drank white wine. I knew my next partner would be a beer drinker.

Livermore Valley Citizens

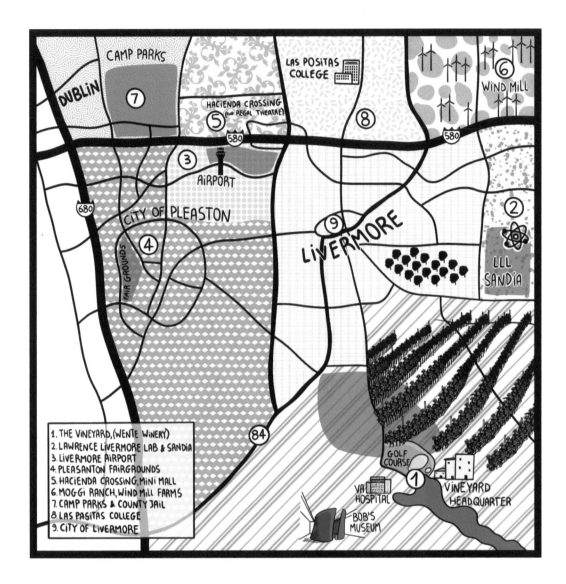

Chapter 38
The Townships

1. **The Wente Estate Vineyard and Golf Course:** Located at the end of Arroyo Road, will be renamed the "Vineyard." It consists of a winery, restaurant, golf course, champagne caves, numerous warehouses, and 1,600 acres of grapes.

2. **Lawrence Livermore National Laboratory and Sandia:** The lab consists of 500 acres, 170 buildings, three machine shops, and two biological labs. Next to the Lab is Sandia National-al Laboratory. It has three facilities, including a machine shop, enclosed by high-security fencing around the entire 400 acres. This area will be farmed for opium poppies and to manufacture medicines. Opium will be bartered for other goods and services.

3. **Livermore Municipal Airport:** 644 acres with a 5,253 feet long runway. 105 airplanes, two helicopters 400 hangars, and Beeb's restaurant. The tower will be secured 24-7 by guards armed with Barrett rifles, rifles with a range of two miles. The Highway traffic control sign

"Amber Alert" will now read, "Hwy 580 is a toll road, exit at Airport Blvd and park at Beeb's restaurant." Commuters will, depending on their business in the Valley, be required to pay a toll.

4. **Pleasanton/Alameda County Fairgrounds:** 76 buildings, including barns for cattle, sheep, goats, and racehorses. There's a racetrack and a 9-hole golf course. The fairgrounds will host a weekly produce market and a monthly flea market.

5. **Hacienda Crossing:** A mini-mall with numerous stores, Home Goods, Whole Foods, Starbucks, Best Buy, Barnes & Noble, Bed Bath and Beyond, Old Navy, Chipotle, Living Spaces, Sharma Dental, and a Shell Gas Station. If you need gasoline, you just pull into a station and fill your car. If you need shoes, there's Nordstrom's, Nordstrom's Rack, and countless other stores. Just try on a pair you like and wear them back to the Vineyard.

6. **Moggi Ranch:** Located in the Altamont Hills has over 800 trees. Most of the fruit will be picked, crushed, fermented, and distilled into brandies called Eau de vies, products that can be bartered for other goods and services. Similar to other farms, Moggi will provide milk, dairy products, eggs, dried fruit, nuts, and olive oil for its citizens. The location of the Moggi farm will not be publicized to protect it from marauders.

7. **Camp Parks Military Training Facility and County Jail:** Secure storage for military vehicles and weapons.

8. **Las Positas College:** Supplemental Fairground classes with Vocational Education Classes including dental hygiene.

9. **City of Livermore:** With resources of Dom's Surplus, Costco, Lowe's, Home Depot, CVS, Rite Aid, Walgreens, Safeway, etc.

Chapter 39
The Nine Commissioners

The resources available to the *Althing* Community are as follows:

- A high-end restaurant, patio covered with wisteria vines. A fully operational winery of 8,000 acres planted in Chardonnay and Cabernet Sauvignon vines.

- An 18-hole golf course with full bar with a large selection of wine and draft beer.

- Two 3-acre vegetable gardens with more available farmable land.

- Organic orchards of almond, olive, peach, plum, and pecan trees.

- A wedding chapel.

- An outdoor concert facility, seating 300.

- Champagne caves for private events.

- A corporate yard with tools to repair trucks, tractors, and golf carts.

- Access to numerous wine warehouses.

- Electricity will be provided from the Wind Farms on Flynn Road.

- Water for the Vineyard will come from numerous deep wells and Lake Del Valle.

Commissioner of the Livermore Airport

This person will oversee all incoming and outbound flights in the Livermore Valley. They will provide security for the airplane hangars and storage facilities. The hangars will serve as storage for food supplies such as flour, sugar, salt, rice, and coffee beans. Hangar #3 will serve as a large walk-in smoker for meats. All hangars will run with security cameras for as long as they are operational.

Commissioner of Viticulture

They will be responsible for the Wente grape vineyards and another 27 or so smaller Livermore wineries along East Avenue and Tesla Road. They will also be responsible for the care of vineyards which includes watering, pruning, harvesting, crushing, and fermentation. The commissioner will produce and bottle wine.

Commissioner of Defense

His mandate is to secure and protect the nine townships in Livermore Valley. The minister will have a staff of five and numerous cars, trucks, and small arms to protect the region.

- Protect Home Depot, Target, Walmart, Ace Hardware, Lowe's and other supply stores.

- Secure food supplies at Costco, Safeway, Lucky's, and numerous other smaller markets.

- Keep looters away from the liquor stores Total Wine and BevMo.

- Provide 24 hour security for all drugstores, including CVS, Walmart, Rite Aid, and Walgreen's.

Many locations listed above have security cameras. We expect these cameras will stop working after a few months. Patrol of the Livermore Valley to keep people safe and keep out looters will be the responsibility of the Commissioner of Defense.

Commissioner of Homeland Security (The Vineyard)

He will oversee daily activities at the Vineyard. This includes security, food, and lodging for everyone living at the Vineyard.

He will screen new community arrivals and provide them with food, housing, and transportation. They will remove individuals not found fit to become a member of the immediate community.

Commissioner of Deprivation

Acts as the game warden and will be equipped with a pump-action Remington rifles to keep deer and feral pigs out of the Vineyard. He can also, at will, shoot turkeys, rabbits, raccoons, and feral cats. Larger animals such as deer and pigs will be made into sausage, smoked, or made into jerky. He will also provide water for the cattle roaming around Camp Parks.

Commissioners to be appointed

Baking, Transportation, Regional Parks, Libraries, Recycling, Education, Gardens, Family Counselor, Breeding of Small Animals, Horse and Cattle Breeding.

Chapter 40

The Coffee Roaster

I was talking to Rod and asked him to hold on for a few minutes. I had just seen Dan Hicks walk through the front door of Buffalo Bill's, and I knew he was looking for me.

I told Dan that with the Buffalo Bill virus survivors, I was forming a community based on a Viking-style government. Dan's face had a blank look. He didn't want to be troubled trying to understand the concept of a Viking Village. I had a long history with Dan. He worked for me as an assistant brewer, and I'd fired him because of his know-it-all attitude. Plus, he had the1960s hippie shaggy look that I hated.

I decided to send Dan on a wild goose chase. I told him to get a U-Haul truck and drive to San Jose and get me a coffee roasting machine. I wanted to roast my own beans for a Russian Imperial Coffee Stout. I didn't mention that he would need a forklift to put the coffee roaster in the back of the truck, and the roaster weighs 2,800 pounds.

I gave Dan my cell phone number and said, "If you need help, call me."

After he left, I blocked his number.

I went back to my meeting with Rod and suggested we meet at Starbucks in San Ramon before heading to Walnut Creek and then on to Concord Naval Base.

I watched Rod speed off on his Harley. Ten minutes later, Tony and I jumped into a Wagoner and headed to San Ramon.

When we got to Starbucks, I saw Rod was already sitting at a table talking to a young woman. I sat at their table, interrupted the conservation, and started asking her questions.

"What's your name?"

"Liz"

"And where do you live?" I asked.

"I live in Hayward and work at the Funky Monkey."

"How did you get here?"

"I walked from Hayward," she said.

"Where are you going?"

"I'm looking for a safe place to live."

I changed the subject and asked, "What's your favorite beer?"

With a big smile, she responded, "Flat Tire Amber Ale!"

I smiled back and said, "Great, you're a beer drinker."

I told her I was in the process of setting up a "Village" with virus survivors at the Wente Winery in Livermore.

Liz looked at me and announced, "I'd be an excellent addition to the Village. I can cook and shoot a Glock 19." I explained to her that Viking law didn't require guns to keep societal order.

Liz interrupted me, pointed a finger at Rod, and said, "I want a ride on his Harley."

I asked Rod, "Do you want a passenger?

"Sure," Rod responded, "She doesn't look like a wolf in sheep's clothing to me."

I looked at her sternly and said, "I can deal with women who are vegetarians. Drink Pellegrino bottled water and get $120 hair cuts. I'm just a bit afraid of a woman who can shoot a Glock."

Liz said, "I'm easy to get along with, low maintenance, eat everything, even peanuts, and have good teeth. I really want to join the Village."

Rod interrupted the conversation, saying. "Hey, she loves motorcycles and has good teeth. What more could you ask for?"

I watched Rod and Liz speed off, heading north towards Walnut Creek.

Tony and I followed in the Wagoneer. When we got close to Walnut Creek, the Garmin GPS came on.

In six miles, exit onto South Main St. In a 1/2 mile, take a left on Sycamore. Take a left on Locust. You now have arrived. Peet's Coffee is on the right.

Once there Liz, was already behind the counter making an espresso. She looked up and explained, "I used to be a barista at Peet's."

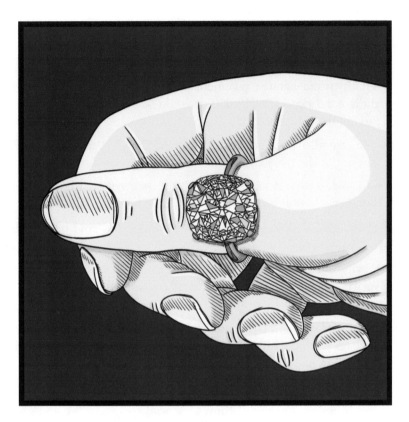

Chapter 41

Lunch at Tiffany's

I stepped outside and used my cell to call Dan Hicks.

"Hey Dan, we're at Sam's Chowder House on Highway 1, three miles north of Half Moon Bay. Join us. The clam chowder is great."

I made a second call to my friend Wayne in Walnut Creek and said, "I'm having coffee at Peet's on Locust Avenue. Join me."

Ten minutes later, Wayne showed up in his Land Rover. I explained over coffee that I was forming a community based on the Viking *Althing* government. Wayne mentioned he'd seen a PBS documentary on the Vikings. He wanted to be the Village "lögsögu-madr" or ombudsman, settling arguments over property rights.

I changed the subject by suggesting we grab some shopping carts from Whole Foods and hit Macy's. I wanted some Dockers, 501 Levis, and Ecco shoes.

An hour later, we pushed our carts out of Macy's. Wayne said, "Hey, there's a new Tiffany's store on South Main Street. It's so ritzy that the roof drain pipes are made from titanium."

I said, "Let's go! Tiffany's is full of great stuff!"

Wayne answered, "Hey, maybe with jewelry, we can find women to join the *Althing*."

I answered, "Not many women drink craft beer."

I stopped outside Tiffany's, tossed the Dockers on the sidewalk, and walked into the store. I started filling my cart with trays of Rolex watches, pearl necklaces, and broaches. The fourth layer was a tray of loose diamonds.

I looked at a flashy seven-karat engagement ring in a display case and wondered if Tiffany's sold real diamond rings for $18,000. It could be made from zirconia, and no one would be able to tell the difference.

Then I saw one case filled with gold bricks. I broke the glass and took all of the bricks. I pushed the cart out of the store and loaded up the Wagoneer.

When we returned, Rod and Liz were finishing their coffee. Liz looked up and remarked that the week-old muffins still tasted fresh.

Rod watched me load the Wagoneer with the jewelry and gold bricks. He inquired, "Where did you get the gold?"

I told him Wayne and I walked into Tiffany's and helped ourselves. Rod was a jeweler by trade and very envious of our Tiffany's score. He then cursed me for not telling him that Tiffany's was just two blocks away.

Rod and Liz jumped on his Harley and disappeared. Thirty minutes later they were back with saddlebags stuffed with watches and jewelry from James Allen and the Shane Company. I noticed Liz had a large diamond ring on her thumb.

Rod, not saying a word, sped off with Liz on the back of his Harley.

I waited fifteen minutes and said, "Tony, let's head to Livermore and check out the Wente Winery."

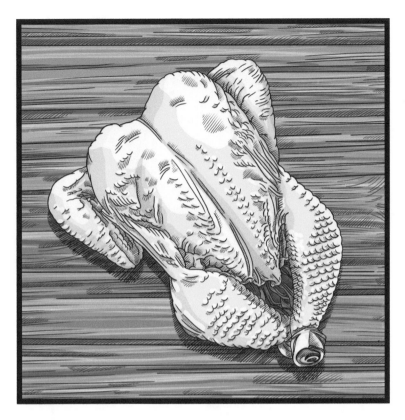

Chapter 42

Rhode Island Red

Tony parked the Wagonner next to the restaurant patio. I could see Mitch at the barbecue pit. Standing next to him was a woman with big hips. She drew my attention because I recognized that body. It was my ex-girlfriend, Linda. I wondered if she was still mad at me because I didn't take her to the Met in New York.

On the back of the patio was a sign reading, *Tonight Hootie and the Blowfish! General Admission $50, Front Row Seats $300.*

I asked Mitch, "Is there still Green Pea soup in the refrigerator?"

He answered loudly, "How in the hell did you know that?"

"The GPS told me," I responded. I kept an eye out for the U-Haul truck and Dan Hicks. I was sure he'd be on his way to Half Moon Bay for clam chowder. I hoped he didn't find out we were really in Livermore.

Tony and I sat at a patio table talking, and soon Mitch joined us.

I asked, "What's for dinner?"

"I roasted a couple of Rhode Island Reds."

"Did you find them in the freezer?"

"No, these are freshly killed."

Again I asked, "Where did you find the chickens?

117

Taking off his A's baseball cap, Mitch placed it over his heart and said. "I found them at the Kiddie Academy School on Vasco Road."

"What?" I exclaimed.

"No one had fed or given them water for days."

"Mitch, how could you kill chickens from a Christian School?"

"It was easy. I used a meat cleaver and cut off their heads."

I asked, "Are you cooking using a Texas BBQ Sauce?"

Mitch answered," Nope, I made a Cajun rub with paprika, cayenne, garlic powder, black pepper, red sea salt, and oregano."

While we talked, Mitch cut two Spanish onions in half. He rubbed them with ground peppercorn butter and placed them face down on the grill.

An hour later, as promised, we had roasted chicken, Caesar salad, pumpkin risotto, and grilled onions for dinner. Dessert was a seven-layer chocolate cake with ice cream. We washed it all down, consuming a bottle of white wine and some New Belgium beer.

The next day I sent Tony up the hill to the VA hospital. I told him to use rubber tires to build a fire. I wanted to create black smoke to signal that we were here.

It worked. Around noon two cars and a pick-up truck showed up at the VA hospital. It was a caravan of survivors from the Dust Bowl Brewery in Turlock.

We took them down hill to the Wente Winery and sat on the patio. I explained that our fledgling democracy was based on the Viking way of life called the *Althing*. I showed them around the restaurant, winery, and golf course, and of course, they all wanted to become citizens.

I asked Tony to interview everyone and have them sign the pledge. At the end of the day, the Village had grown to 28 people.

Everyone would need a place to live, so we formed a car caravan and checked out the homes along Arroyo Road. These weren't ordinary tract homes. Every home had at least five bedrooms and four full bathrooms.

Some of the larger homes had ten rooms, six bathrooms, and a TV room with a 72-inch plasma. When you entered the kitchen, the lights automatically came on, as did a small TV featuring a Martha Stewart cooking program. Most kitchens had an 8-burner Wolf Range. All had double-door refrigerators with a TV screen and ice maker built into the doors. Some homes had a built-in brick pizza oven.

These McMansions all had double door garages full of the usual items: washer and dryer, a freezer/refrigerator combo, bicycles, camping equipment, and some had small swordfish boats.

I opened the door of one of the garage refrigerators and found it full of Omaha steaks. The only thing of actual value in the garage was two propane tanks. The only problem with selecting a home was that many contained the bones of a family that was killed by the virus. The group decided, for security, to live close to one another and picked houses on a cul-de-sac. I opted to live in a mobile home park near the rodeo grounds.

The most useful store in downtown Livermore was Dom's Surplus. It had all manner of survival items, from guns to metal detectors to emergency survival food, items that couldn't be found at Home Depot or Costco.

Chapter 43

Suburbia

I had chosen to have the *Althing* members move to Livermore Valley for several reasons.

First, I'd lived in the city of Livermore in the 1970s. At that time, I was a newspaper photographer and knew the cities of Livermore, Pleasanton, and Dublin like the back of my hand. It was home. I knew everyone from the mayor to the lifeguards at Shadow Cliff.

Second, in the late 1930s, my parents met in Livermore. At the time, my mom was working at a tuberculosis sanitarium. My dad worked on the construction of Highway 580 over the Altamont Pass, connecting the highway to Stockton and Sacramento, CA.

I remember my mom pointing out a Quonset hut that was now an antique store in Livermore. She'd told me that my dad had Apartment #7, where I was conceived.

Third, thirty years later, my new wife Janet and I visited Livermore on our honeymoon. I remember drinking white wine at the Cresta Blanca Winery. I decided not to show Janet the Quonset hut where I was conceived.

In the 1980s, the Wente Winery family bought the Cresta Blanca winery and put 22 million dollars into modernizing the place. They added a two-star Michelin restaurant, a concert facility, and an 18-hole golf course. The old Cresta Blanca was renamed the Wente Vineyard and Golf Course.

The land around the winery is certified as an Audubon Cooperative Sanctuary. They restored and expanded the old Cresta Blanca sandstone caves to meet OSHA standards, and under the cottonwood trees, they constructed a wedding chapel.

The concert area next to the restaurant had seating for 1,700 people. Front-row seats at the Linda Ronstadt concert had gone for as high as $1,000.

I had some of the Foxfire back-to-the-land books: *Build a log cabin, Churning your own Butter* and *Basic Basket Making*. When the time came, we would plant deer grass in the sand traps at the golf course and take up Indian basket weaving.

Inside the restaurant near the men's toilet door, I hung the sign General Manager's Office. The door led outside to the golf course.

Chapter 44
Breakfast on the Patio

It was 7 a.m., and the sun was up. Tony and I sat on the patio, drinking our first cappuccinos and discussing the to-do list.

Mitch saw us on the patio and 15 minutes later showed up with two biscuit egg sandwiches. On the side were French bread, Irish butter, and Martha Stewart's peach jam. I asked Mitch, "Where did you find the French bread?" He had been waiting for the chance to talk about his baking skills. "I found a sourdough starter in the fridge, mixed it with 3 cups of flour and 1-2/3 cups of warm water. I worked the dough for ten minutes and put it back in the fridge to rest and rise overnight. This morning I let the dough warm up, worked it into loaves, and let them rise for an hour. The loaves were baked at 400 degrees for 30 minutes."

I asked, "Mitch, how long can you, with the supplies that are in the restaurant, feed our group before we run out of essentials?"

He responded, "We have at least 100 pounds of rice and flour, four bags of potatoes, and three flats of eggs. There's a side of beef hanging in the walk-in cooler, two freezers full of pork and lamb chops, ducks, geese, capons, quail, and a couple of Rocky Free Range turkeys. We have plenty of food and vegetables in the garden. In a couple of weeks, milk and eggs will be a problem, but I think there is a farm in the Altamont Hills where we can barter wine for milk and eggs. I figure I can feed everyone for a couple of months. Don't forget I can always make a run to Walmart and get anything we need."

"Good to know. Can I have another cappuccino? How much coffee does the restaurant have?" Mitch said, "We have enough beans for a couple of months. Didn't you send someone to get a coffee roaster?"

I made a mental note to send Tony to get coffee beans at every grocery store and coffee shop in the Valley. With luck, we would have enough beans to last a year. Without luck, Dan Hicks would show up with the U-Haul.

Mitch noted, "If electricity fails, we have backup solar, and at Home Depot, I picked up two gas generators for electricity."

I pointed out that electricity and water for the Livermore Valley come from the Hetch Hetchy Dam near Yosemite Valley. I was sure that the power grid was good for a few months. I asked Tony to look into connecting to the Altamont windmills. I knew we would need our own electrical system for the tower at the airport and the warehouses that store our food supplies.

en.wikipedia.org/wiki/Altamont_Pass_wind_farm

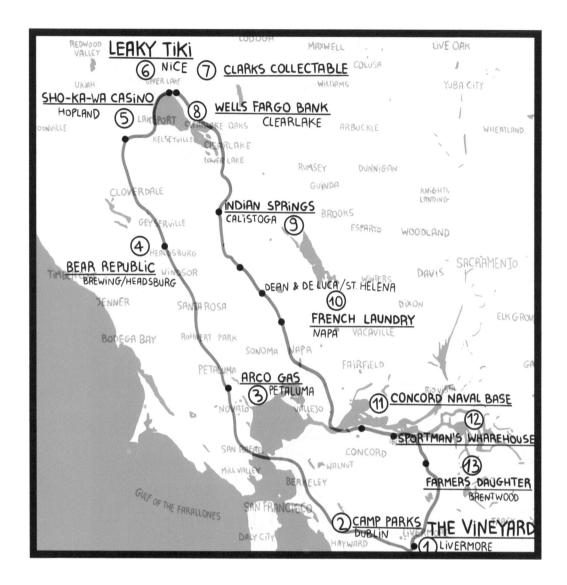

Chapter 45
Road Trip

I told Tony to get the Wagoneer ready for a road trip to Clearlake.

"Why Clearlake?" He asked. I responded by saying. "Last summer, I met a woman at the Turf Club, and after a couple of drinks, she told me a story about a stash of gold bricks at the Wells Fargo Bank in Clearlake."

At the time, she was the Assistant Manager at the bank and had helped a local farmer open a large safe deposit box. It seems he was leasing land to gold prospectors and over the years had sold the same claim over and over again. In doing so, he bought bars of gold and she helped him deposit the gold into the bank's vault.

Suddenly last year, he was arrested and charged with fraud. He was salting the ground with "fools gold." The week before he was to go to prison, she heard he had fled to South America and was sure the Wells Fargo Bank vault had hundreds of the gold bricks.

When I was in high school, my dad purchased mining rights on federal land near Auburn, California. Then after graduation, I spent one summer with a pick and shovel digging in his mine. We never found the gold-quartz vein he was looking for…

As soon as I heard the Wells Fargo story, I wanted to do a road trip to Clearlake Wells Fargo and get those gold bricks.

I had books on gold, *A History of Gold and Money The Power of Gold The California Gold Rush*. I love gold brick and coins and had read about the Spanish conquistadors killing the leader of the Incas and taking tons of gold back to the King of Spain. There's a reason the Egyptians and Mayans worshipped gold. It has power over people. I already had taken a bag of gold bars from Tiffany's, and I wanted more.

I knew we could barter wine for food, but with gold bricks, we could get the things we needed for long-term survival.

That morning at 9 a.m., with Tony at the wheel of the Wagoneer, we left for Clearlake. When we passed through downtown Livermore, the Garmin GPS kicked on and announced:

"In a quarter-mile, use the left lane and enter Highway 580 West."

An hour later, we were on the San Rafael Bridge, and I could see smoke rising in the distance in several areas. I wondered why we couldn't all get along.

I knew other California breweries with virus survivors would form their own communities. I just hoped they would form democratic or colonial governments and join together as free states like the United States had in 1776. I sort of doubted that it would happen soon. I didn't think any other breweries would create a Viking *Althing* government.

Living off the land with a vegetable garden, a couple of cows, and few chickens doesn't feed very many people. In five years, when the sugar, salt, flour, and rice at Target and Costco are used up, getting food would become a real problem for every community. We needed to stock as much wine and gold as we could. I knew that in a few years, we would be bartering for meat, sugar, and salt.

The Garmin directed us onto Highway 101 North and let us know it was four miles to the Arco station in Petaluma. It gave an estimated arrival time in Clearlake of two hours and twenty minutes. I'd hoped we would make it there by noon but now knew that wouldn't happen.

At the Arco Station, the employees were gone, so topping off the Wagoneer gas tank was easy. Inside the station, we helped ourselves to five-day-old hot dogs and some Cokes. I grabbed a few Starbucks Frappuccinos for later. I knew that if I chugged a 16-ounce drink, I'd have to pull over to pee within twenty minutes.

The gas station coolers that lined the back wall of the station had everything from Red Bull to cold Bud. We helped ourselves to cases of Sierra Nevada Pale Ale and Lagunitas IPA. Drinking and driving was not a problem for me. I remembered enjoying the feel of a Mickey's Big Mouth bottle between my legs.

The Garmin took us to the town of Hopland, and we stopped at the Mendocino Brewery. I went inside and found the place was empty. I grabbed a couple of cases of Red Tail Ale and left.

en.wikipedia.org/wiki/Mendocino_Brewing_Company

"In two miles, turn right onto Highway 157 and drive six miles. The Sho-Ka-Wah Casino will be on your left," the Garmin said.

www.hoplandtribe.com

The casino was self-contained, with solar panels, two wells, four windmills, and a state-of-the-art sewage-treatment plant. California state law prohibited new buildings from emitting pollution of any kind.

The casino parking lot attendant pointed us to visitor's parking. I found it ironic that the parking spaces for the handicapped were full of new cars. I thought to myself: the disabled and American Indians are doing all right. They keep money in circulation, eating, drinking, and gambling.

The casino was packed. People were gambling as if the world had not ended. I noticed craft beers were cheap at $3.00. I saw the casino was full of beer drinkers. I was sure the employees were drinking beer during their breaks. Gamblers were singly focused on winning. I wasn't even sure they cared about winning money beyond placing the next bet. They no longer cared about the outside world.

It was Monday, and the Casino restaurant's special was a Steak-N-Lobster dinner for $12.95 along with a complimentary glass of beer. People were eating lobsters, burgers, steaks, and drinking beer. A giant wall of televisions were re-broadcasting the last Super Bowl.

After an hour at the casino, we headed up Highway 29 towards Lakeport. We turned left on Highway 20 and soon arrived in the town of Nice. The only tourist attraction in town was Clarke's Lunch Box Museum.

www.roadsideamerica.com/tip/23037

The Garmin kicked on again: *"In one mile, on your left is 4220 East Highway 20. You will have arrived at your final destination, Wells Fargo Bank."*

We stopped and looked at a pile of rubble that used to be the Wells Fargo Bank. Someone with a bulldozer had demolished the bank and removed the vault. The gold was gone. Our trip to Clearlake was a bust.

Chapter 46
The Leaky Tiki Tavern

When we left the bank parking lot, I programmed the Garmin to 2535 Lakeshore Boulevard, the home of the Leaky Tiki Tavern.

On the wall behind the bar was a sign that read: *Welcome to the home of the Low-Life Club.*

The beer selection was simple…Corona, Miller Lite, and Budweiser long neck. Behind the bar, I could see 12-ounce cans of Pabst Blue Ribbon.

The sign on the door to the men's room announced *Toilet Broke, Use Ladies.* Inside on the sink was a tiny bar of soap, and a half of a roll of Kirkland paper towels sat on the back of the women's room sink. The handwritten note said, "Do not throw paper towels into the toilet."

Near the pool table on the back wall were photographs of the damage from the 1968 winter flood that closed the bar for three days. One photo showed ducks swimming under the pool table. The flood gave visitors and regulars something to talk about. I grabbed a case of Pabst and headed to the Motel 6.

We spent the evening drinking and eating potato chips.

motel6.com

In the morning, I set the Garmin for Livermore and the Wente Winery. It instructed us: *"It's 120 miles to the Wente Vineyards. Take highway 20 to Calistoga. Turn left on Highway 29. Go south toward Napa."*

My cell rang, and it was Mitch. He was checking in on us and asked, "How're things going?" I avoided the question and said, "With luck, we'll be back tonight so save some dinner for us." Mitch asked again, "What about the gold bricks?"

I had to tell him the truth. When we got to the Bank, it just was a pile of rubble, and the vault was gone. I wondered if the woman at the Turf Club was lying to me about the gold bricks. I again changed the conversation. "What's for dinner?"

Mitch changed his tone to that of a waiter at a high-end San Francisco Bistro, saying proudly, "Seared prosciutto-wrapped asparagus, gorgonzola polenta, rabbit braised in pinot noir, a spinach or a dill cucumber salad with yogurt-mint dressing. Dessert will be bourbon chocolate cake topped with heavy cream and granulated sugar. The espresso is Peet's Jamaican blend".

I asked sarcastically, "Did you get the rabbits at Kinder Care Day Center?" He said, "No, I found USDA rabbits in the freezer," I asked again. "Is there enough rabbit to feed 27 people?" Mitch answered," No, so I had to catch stray cats. I'm marinating both in white Balsamic vinegar. I'm sure that after a few bottles of wine, no one will be able to tell the difference between cats and rabbits."

"Mitch, are you joking about the stray cats?" I asked. "Ok, I didn't kill any cats, but this morning I did see some turkeys in the vineyard."

Our next stop on Hwy 17 was the Rutherford Winery. We sat in the courtyard and drank award-winning Peju wines and Lagunitas IPA.

We talked about the Leaky Tiki and how my hunt for gold bars was a bust.

I defended myself: "Never trust what a woman in a bar tells you."

We pushed on south and arrived at my favorite delicatessen, Dean and Delucca's. I was in a hurry to use the men's room. While there, we loaded the Wagoneer with Ethiopian organic coffee, chocolate chip cookies, olive tapenade, wines, and whiskies. Not left behind were bamboo cutting boards and a set of German Wüsthof knives. By now, I must have four sets of Wüsthof Knives. On our way out the door, I took the hand-forged silver egg poaching spoons.

Our next stop was The French Laundry. It's the most famous restaurant in the Napa Valley, has three Michelin Stars, and is considered by Anthony Bourdain to be "The Best Restaurant in the world, period." A pre-set fixe dinner boasts seven courses plus dessert

and would have set you back a mere $300. That doesn't include wine, and the cheapest glass was $35.

I opened the front door and walked around an empty restaurant. I tried to figure out what to take. Besides a fancy hand-painted bowl, I ended up taking a couple of Italian hams and a few jars of pickled red onions.

frenchlaundry.com

Back on the road, the Garmin kicked on and announced 22 miles to the Concord Naval Weapons Station.

In 1944 a ship being loaded with ammunition exploded. The sound of the explosion was heard in San Francisco, some 18 miles away. It killed 320 sailors, marines, and hundreds of dockworkers, most of whom were African-American.

When we arrived at the Naval Base, the gate was wide open. We drove down to the waterfront and, with no one around, the place felt eerie. We cruised around the munitions bunkers and warehouses. Everything was wide open and empty. Then I saw the sign "Warning Hazardous Materials" and decided it was time to leave.

Next, we made two quick stops. First was the Sportsman's Warehouse in Brentwood, and then Cabella's World of Camping. I wanted to pick up some lightweight weapons, like deer rifles, shotguns, bows, and arrows. I grabbed a couple of pairs of size nine of Brunello Cucinelli hiking boots and two mountain bicycles.

The bicycles were securely tied down using multi-colored mountaineer rope on top of the Wagoneer. We headed towards Livermore when the Garmin came on again: "*Take Highway 4 South to Vasco Road.*"

We passed numerous abandoned almond and cherry tree orchards but didn't stop.

Chapter 47
Vineyard

Thirty minutes later, the Garmin announced: *"Take Livermore exit left on Arroyo Road. Go three miles to the Wente Vineyards Restaurant Visitors Center. The golf course opens at 6:00 a.m., and daily wine tasting is from 10 a.m. to 6 p.m. The restaurant opens at 11:00. The soup of the day is Green Pea garnished with smoked Italian ham."*

Around 5 p.m., we arrived back at the Vineyard.

Mitch saw us, came out to the patio, and announced, "Dinner will be ready in about an hour. "

Once dinner was over, we held the first *Althing* meeting. A vote was taken, and as the founder of the *Althing*, I was chosen to be the "Godord," The Godord term would be for one year.

The next item of discussion was to change the name of the "Wente Family Estate." We chose for our village to be called simply "The Vineyard."

As the newly elected Godord, I appointed commissioners to oversee the townships.

Soon, because everyone at the meeting was drinking, no more governmental items were discussed. We all agreed that no *Althing* meeting should be longer than 90 minutes. This rule was later changed to three days. We were having too much fun.

Chapter 48

Dr. Bob's Museum of Modern Art

My cell phone rang early the next morning. It was Dr. Bob, a radiologist and art collector. He'd heard I was creating a village at the Wente Winery in Livermore. Dr. Bob was very familiar with the area because he had worked at the VA Hospital, just up the hill from the Wente Winery.

Dr. Bob wanted me to help him convert the Veteran's Hospital into an art museum. He also wanted to change the name of the hospital to "The Robert Shimshak Museum.

Bob said, "I'll go to the MOMA, the Palace of the Legion of Art and the de Young Museum and take a couple of Jackson Pollock and Gerhard Richter works for the museum."

Bob also wanted to use the lawn area of the Hospital and create an outdoor sculpture garden. He also wanted to paint the walls of the VA hospital to look like the French prehistoric caves at Lascaux.

I explained again that we needed an 18 wheeler truck with a crane to move the Rodin sculpture pieces. Bob was ignoring me, so I raised my voice and said, "Bob, how are *you* going to move a 17-ton Richard Serra sculpture?"

He replied, "I need your help on this one. I know there's a way to do it."

The real problem was that no one in the village knew how to drive an 18-wheeler truck.

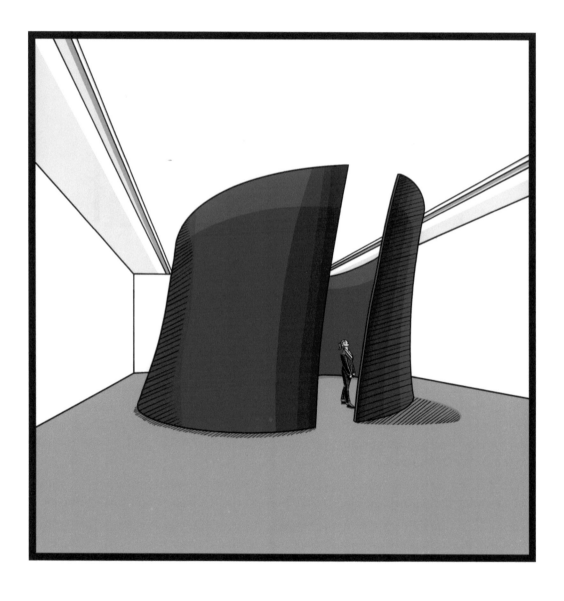

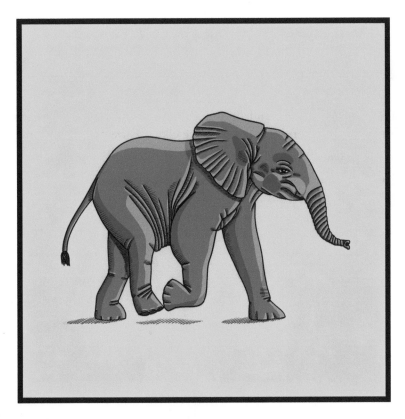

Chapter 49
Baby Back Elephant Ribs

The next day I received a call from Steve, who said he lived in Danville and had heard about the Village and the *Althing* community. Steve mentioned that someone had released all the animals, including the elephants, from the Oakland Zoo.

Those elephants had tramped over the hills to Danville. They were at the Eugene O'Neill House and having their fill of roses and fruit trees.

Steve asked me, "Do your want the elephants? One of them is a baby."

I said, "I'll take the baby."

My cell rang. It was Rod saying he had a change of heart about becoming a citizen. He and Liz would definitely sign the loyalty pledge.

Rod asked, "How hard could that be? What do we need to prove we will be good citizens?" An idea popped into my head, and I said, "Rob, if you and Liz shoot the elephant without complaining, I will make sure you are welcomed into the community."

Rod said, "How hard could it be? What is it?"

I asked, "Rod, do you have a gun big enough to shoot an elephant?"

"No, but I know where I can get an AK47."

"Rod, I don't want you to murder an elephant. I just want you to shoot it." Liz was listening to our conversation and chimed in, "I want to shoot an elephant!" "Rod," I said, "You have to tell Liz that an elephant has a thick skull, and she should plan on shooting it behind the ear. Rod, you have to tell her it's a baby elephant!"

The phone was quiet for a minute, and Rod responded, "We both want to be part of the community. Liz will watch, and I'll shoot the elephant." Rod, your Danville contact person, is Steven. He'll meet you at the Danville Clock Tower today at noon. He will take you to the elephants. And one more thing, no drinking on the job."

I could tell that Rod wasn't excited about what I was asking him to do. He asked, "Will there be anything else, Chief?"

"Yes, you will need a U-Haul with a winch to move the elephant onto the truck. Oh, one more thing. Swing by Home Depot and pick up a Makita chainsaw. You will need to gut the elephant before loading it into the U-Haul."

It occurred to me that female elephants can be pretty protective of their young, and shooting a baby may be a problem. Rod might end up shooting all three elephants. I hoped the AK-47 could do the job.

I now turned to Tony and asked, "Can you do me a big favor?"

"Sure, what do you need?"

I said, "Go to the tool shed and get the backhoe and meet me on the first green of the golf course."

I got there first. Tony arrived ten minutes later with the backhoe.

He then asked, "Now, what do you want me to do?"

I answered. "I need you to dig a fire pit. It has to be six feet wide, nine feet long, and five feet deep."

The pit was (6 + 9 + 5 = 20). Was it just a coincidence that twenty was the number of days since the release of NOFI?

Tony asked me, "What's this pit for?" I explained, "We were going to build a Hawaiian underground oven called an Imu. We're making the pit big enough to cook an elephant."

I told Tony, "When you're finished digging the pit, go to Safeway and get four or five boxes of fireplace logs and some lighter fluid. While you're driving around Livermore, look for rocks. You know, the rocks that people use to decorate their yard. And, look for banana trees. If you can't find any, go to Alden Lane Nursery. I know they have banana trees. Plus, I need to stop at Dom's Surplus. I need burlap bags and a canvas tarp."

I could hear Tony mutter out of the side of his mouth, "You're crazy"

Chapter 50
The Hawaiian Imu

The process of creating an underground Hawaiian oven called an Imu was described to me by Keanu Halfpenny, a Hawaiian guy who now lives in Detroit. His given name was Liki Hapahaneri. Over the years, I kept his handwritten instructions.

Items needed for the Imu:

- Shovels
- Lava rock
- Broomsticks
- Burlap bags
- Large canvas
- Lighter fluid
- Red Alaea Salt
- Banana leaves from several trees and the trunk of one tree

1. Dig a pit wide and deep enough to bury a baby elephant. Pile the dirt well away from the pit to make it easy to shovel it back over the elephant.

2. Crumple newspapers and use a large amount of kindling for the fire pit. Insert two broom handles, creating air vents at both ends of the pit. Mix together layers of logs and lava rocks.

3. Fill the pit 3/4 full with layers of logs and rocks.

4. Remove the broomsticks and pour lighter fluid or kerosene down the stick holes. Light the fluid using match sticks. Step back. Smoke will come out of the broomstick holes.

5. Allow the fire to slowly burn for a couple of hours, heating the rocks. During this time, use water to soak the burlap bags and canvas.

6. Prepare the elephant by rubbing it inside and out with the coarse salt. First, however, use the chainsaw and remove the elephant's feet and tie his trunk to a front leg. Use a forklift to lift the elephant and place it on a section of a chainlink fence.

7. Using rakes and working quickly, make a shallow depression in the rock bed to place the elephant. Now line the bed with wet banana leaves and then cover them with wet burlap bags.

8. Using the forklift, place the elephant into the bed, covering it with banana leaves then with a wet burlap tarp. Cover the mound with dirt.

9. Everyone in the group should take turns shoveling the dirt onto the mound. Use a garden hose sprinkling the mound.

10. The mound acts as an underground pressure cooker. Look for escaping steam and add damp dirt to cover those small areas. This is how it is done, and twenty-four hours later, the elephant is ready to eat.

11. The final step is a ceremony. Everyone chants, "Overdone, Overdone!" a reference to the Zen belief that perfection is never attainable and everything is "overdone.".

Then someone handed me a red plastic cup full of beer. I raised it and said, "Cheers, everyone, enjoy your baby back elephant ribs!"

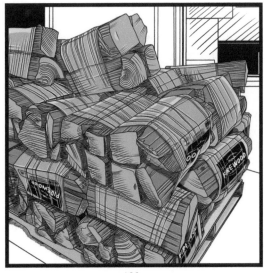

Epilogue

Five years have passed since the infamous elephant barbecue.

The population of the Livermore Valley had grown to 3,551 adults, 1,823 men, 1,502 women, and 152 children. The imbalance between the male and female populations has created social problems. Arranged marriages are becoming the norm.

When our group moved to the Livermore Valley, we formed a Village and chose a decentralized system of government offering a more just and efficient society called the *Althing*. Other communities in Northern California chose democracy, socialism, or oligarchic systems of government. These governments, due to lack of leadership, didn't encourage individual freedoms and entrepreneurship. Now many people, rather than revolting, are moving to the Livermore Valley, and unregistered migrants have become a social problem.

Driving around the Valley these days, you will find many abandoned cars. All have dead Delco or Sears batteries. Ford F-150 pick-up trucks with seven to ten-year extended life batteries, are in high demand.

Because the electrical grid from the windmills has not been maintained, power to homes, businesses, and farms is sporadic. Candle making and the sale of kerosene lamps is now a booming business. East of Livermore on Tesla Road is the abandoned Carnegie Brickworks. In the 1880s, its kilns were fed by the Tesla Coal Mine.

At the Fair Grounds Farm Museum is a coal-fired steam engine. It once produced electricity for the Cities of Livermore and Pleasanton. At a recent township meeting, I brought up the idea, once again, to produce electricity using the steam engine. Everyone liked the idea, but no one wanted to supervise a crew of coal miners.

The water system for the Valley continues to operate because it is gravity-fed from the Hetch Hetchy Dam. All landline telephones are dead. Cell phones work only when the satellite is overhead. On weekends the Fairground hosts a Farmers' Market. It's basically a large swap meet where hundreds of people come together to socialize, buy beer and possibly meet a spouse. The Saturday morning horse auction is an important event and has horse-riding classes. Saddles are in big demand, as is the farrier for shoeing horses.

The 800 car parking lot hosts numerous campers and RVs. Most residents are seasonal, but some with concession stands are permanent residents.

On weekends the concession stands are open with numerous food vendors selling turkey legs, hot dogs, corn dogs, and kettle corn.

The event space, the Farm House, hosts dances, weddings, and community events. A large wood-fired bakery produces rustic breads, focaccia, and cakes.

Several large Texas-style metal ovens are used for barbecuing, smoking meats, and a rotisserie large enough to roast a whole hog or baby elephant.

There are numerous barns for horses and cows and sheds for chickens and pigs. The nine-hole golf course and racetrack have been converted into a cow pasture.

Milk cows produce enough that cheesemaking has become a good business.

The fairgrounds have a covered amphitheater for public meetings and traveling theater groups.

The home economics classes for canning, pickling, and sewing are well attended, as is the one on open pit cooking. Both men and women attend the baking class.

There's also a maintenance area with a woodshop, greenhouse, and mechanical shop where tools can be rented. A public garden hosts a family weekend event. The waiting list for one-quarter of an acre of land is one year.

The Wente Vineyard has developed trade routes for meat, salt, sugar, flour, and eggs. Beer is in high demand, and several towns have reopened micro-breweries. Beer, wine, and spirits bottles are reused. One bottle of beer will get you three bottles of wine. The inventory of wine at the Vineyard is high because there have been three good harvests.

At the Livermore library, I found the book, *Working Horses of Lancaster County*. It illustrates how to hitch draft horses to a plow. The future of power and mobility is clear. I traded five of my Tiffany gold bars and three bottles of whiskey for seven horses. Hitching a horse to a plow is not child's play. A horse, if given the opportunity, will step on your foot or worse kick you.

I think I should have saved my copy of *The Whole Earth Catalog*.

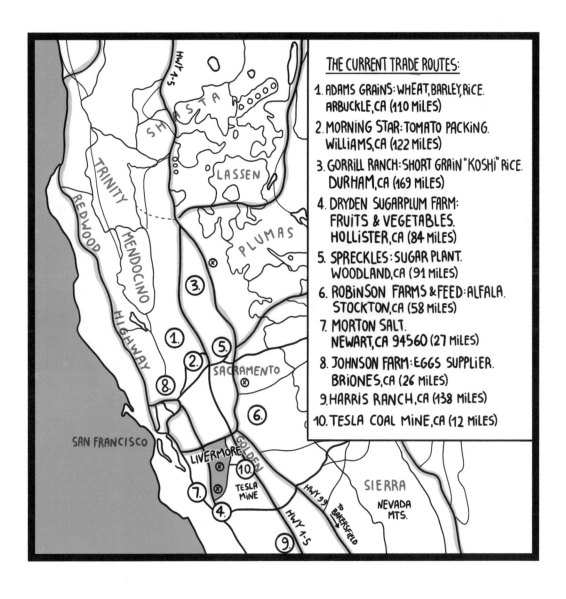

THE CURRENT TRADE ROUTES:

1. ADAMS GRAINS: WHEAT, BARLEY, RICE.
   ARBUCKLE, CA (110 MILES)
2. MORNING STAR: TOMATO PACKING.
   WILLIAMS, CA (122 MILES)
3. GORRILL RANCH: SHORT GRAIN "KOSHI" RICE.
   DURHAM, CA (169 MILES)
4. DRYDEN SUGARPLUM FARM:
   FRUITS & VEGETABLES.
   HOLLISTER, CA (84 MILES)
5. SPRECKLES: SUGAR PLANT.
   WOODLAND, CA (91 MILES)
6. ROBINSON FARMS & FEED: ALFALA.
   STOCKTON, CA (58 MILES)
7. MORTON SALT.
   NEWART, CA 94560 (27 MILES)
8. JOHNSON FARM: EGGS SUPPLIER.
   BRIONES, CA (26 MILES)
9. HARRIS RANCH, CA (138 MILES)
10. TESLA COAL MINE, CA (12 MILES)

Events at the Fair Grounds

Weekend Schedule

Location: Alameda County Fairground Pleasanton

Saturday

8 AM-4 PM ...... Farmers Market - *Ivy Glenn near Front Gate*
8 AM .... Cow Milking Demo, *Cow Barn next to Racing Barn*
8 AM .... Horse Riding - *Racing Barn*
9 AM .... *Althing* Citizenship Class, *Building B*
9 AM .... Cow Care - *Cow Barn next to Racing Barn*
9 AM .... Bee Keeping - *Building A*
9 AM .... Auto maintenance: Car Battery Charging - *Amador Pavilion*
11 AM .... Cooking demonstration: Canning and Pickling - *Amador Pavilion*
11 AM .... Home Economics: Youth Sewing Classes - *California Building*

11 AM ....Chicken Coops Construction - *Fur and Feather Building.*
12 PM................Basic Cooking and Sandwiches, *Subway*
2 PM.................Slaughtering and Butchering Beef - *Building J*
2 PM.................Horse Riding Classes - *Racing Barn*
2 PM.................Dancing Classes - *Young California Building*
3 PM.................*Althing* Citizenship Test, *Building B*
3 PM.................Windmill Service and Repair (Water and Electrical)
4 PM.................Dancing Competition - *Court of the Four Seasons.*
4 PM.................Figure Drawing Classes -*Building R Hobby, Mineral and Gems Building*
5 PM.................Herbal Medicine - *at the old skating rink*
5 PM.................How to Milk a Cow - *Agricultural Building Q*

Sunday
7 AM to 4 PM...Flea Market *Fairground Parking Lot*
8 AM ....Horse Riding - *Racing Barn*

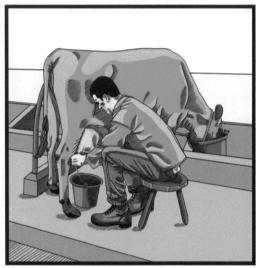

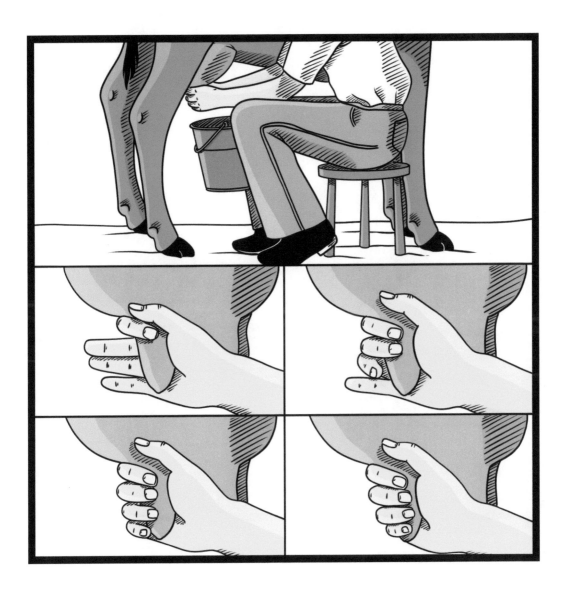

Further Reading

Germs by Judith Miller, Stephen Engelberg, William Broad
Biohazards by Ken Alibeck with Stephen Handelman
How to Rebuild Civilization by Kewis Dartnell
The Anthrax Mutation Alan Scott
Anthrax War: Dead Silence by Eric Nadler Eric & Bob Coen
Spores, Plagues and History: The Story of Anthrax by Chris Home
Anthrax (Deadly Diseases and Epidemics by Janet Decker & Alan Hecht
The Anthrax Protocol: A Dystopian Viral Pandemic Thriller by James Thompson
Dead Silence: Fear and Terror on the Anthrax Trail by Eric Nadler Eric & Bob Coen
Amerithrax: The Hunt for the Anthrax Killer by Robert Graysmith
Robert Koch and the Study of Anthrax by Kathleen Tracy
The Anthrax Mutation by Scott Alan.
Self Sufficiency for the 21st Century by Dick & James Strawbridge
Country Life: Handbook for Realists and Dreamers by Paul Heiney
How to make Biodiesel by John Halle and Dan Thrope
The New Complete book of Self-Sufficiency: Grow All You Can Eat in Three Square Feet by the
Encyclopedia of Herbal Medicine:
The Bee Book by Dorling Kindersley
Encyclopedia of Horse Breeds and Horse Care by Judith Draper
Anthrax War by Bob Coen and Eric Nadler
Five Acres and Independence by M.G.Kains
Self Sufficiency for the 21st Century by Dick & James Strawbridge
How to Make It On the Land by Ray Cohan

And, not to be left off the list: *Keep Chickens! Tending Small Flocks in Cities, Suburbs and Other Small Spaces* by Barbara Kilarski

A necessary book for all of those who survive the pandemic is: *Hand Mending Made Easy: Save Time and Money Repairing Your Own Clothes* by Nan L. Ides

Good Luck

Participants in the Saturday morning Citizenship Classes and Citizenship Test at the Alameda County Fair Ground

Apologies

With apologies to all those people and companies I slandered or whose name is misspelled.

Bank of Boston
Baby Elephant Society
Bellingcat
The Bistro
Boston Red Socks
Brian Glazer
Bob Jones University
Bruce Springsteen
Bikram Yoga
Benny Hinn
Bruuli
Budvar Brewery
Cabala's
Chihuly
Coffeemania, Moscow
Chipotle

Charles Lindbergh
City of Marblehead
City of Boston
City of Livermore
City of Dublin
City of Pleasanton
City of Sverdlovsk
Cornerstone Satellite
CVS
Costco
Delco Battery
Dr. Bentall
Dr. Robert Graham
Dr. Ken Alibek
Dr. Michael Lewis, UC Davis
Dead Frog Report

Don Stewart
Downward Facing Dog
Defon Industries
Disney World
Dockers
Eggo
Estate of Jimmy Swaggart
Eugene O"Neil House
Ecco Shoes
French Laundry
Funky Monkey
Gwyneth Paltrow
Getty Photo
Government of Russia
Genius Sperm Bank
Google

Home Depot
HUGO
Hooters
Home Shopping
Harold Camping
Howard Stern
Imu
Jesus Christ
Joel Osteen
Joyce Meyer
Jim and Tammy Bakker
Jimmy Swagger
Jerry Farwell
Kirby Vacuum
Kenneth Copland
In-N-Out
Joyce Meyers
Joel Osteen
Home Depot
Heaven's Gate
Leaky TiKi Tavern
Ken LaHaye
Krispy Kreme
Kirby Vacuum
L'Abri

Marconi Penguins
McDonald's
Mel Gibson
Macy's
Marshall Applewhite
Martha Stewart
Mary Kay
Marilyn Monroe Estate
Michell Bachman
Mikita Chain Saw
Ned Buntline
Nicole Kidman
Nike
Nordstrom's Rack
Ooh-La-la, Moscow
Pat Robinson
Peptides
Pumpkin Town, SC
Pat Robinson
Pellegrino Water
Readers' Digest
RigScan Monitor
Ron Popeil
Robert Graham
Robert Tilton
Rolex

Sverdlovsk Institute
Sam's Chowder House
Safeway
Starbucks
Stanford University Museum
Selle Italia Bike Saddle
Super 6 Motel
Shane Jewelry Company
Sho-Ka-Wah Casino
Tim LaHaye
Ted Haggard
Tom Cruise
Tom Hanks
The Viking Althing
Tucker Carlson
Thomas Kinkade
Tiffany's
Tour De France
Tri Vita
Target
USDA
Wente Winery
Whole Earth Catalog
Walmart
Walgreens

Sorry if I left anyone off the list…it's just a story.

Disclaimer

The Delco Years is based on many actual events, certain characters, and incidents, both real and imagined. I have provided Wikipedia links to verify those events. The dialogue and events were fictionalized for dramatization. Any similarity to the name of an actual character or history or any person living or dead or actual incident is entirely for dramatic purposes and not intended to reflect on an actual character, history, product, or entity. If you want, blame Ned Buntline.

Thank you

Thank you to everyone who read and proofread this book in progress, especially Nancy Vicknair, Karen Dolan, Geir Jordahl, Tim McKillop, and William Morgan. Special thanks to rare book dealer Ed Smith for his encouragement from the beginning.

Index

No elephants were killed in the writing of this book.

THE DELCO YEARS: A car battery is good for five years
Delco Years Publishing
ISBN: 979-8-9860942-0-5
Copyright 2022
All rights reserved
Bill Owens
Illustrations by Francesca Cosanti
Designed by Kate Jordahl

billowens.com – distilling.com – delcoyears.com

Bill Owens, Ned Buntline and Francesca Cosanti